TASTING

THE WIND

TASTING

THE WIND

Sue A. Lehman

KEYSLIP PRESS

Tasting the Wind © 2012 Sue A. Lehman

KEYSLIP PRESS

Published by KEYSLIP PRESS

http://www.keyslippress.com

ISBN-10: 0983472610

ISBN-13: 978-0-9834726-1-2

Cover Design by Casse Waldman-Forczek

"Whitehead never claimed he built and flew a practical flying machine. He merely stated he built and tested a pair of silken wings and tasted the winds and saw the promise of yet greater machines that would plod the airborne trails of what he described as '...the only Universal Highway.'"

Maj. Wm. J. O'Dwyer, USAF Reserve (Ret.)

TASTING THE WIND

Prologue

Bridgeport, Connecticut, 1912

Henry Andrew Jackson pressed his ear against the barn door, straining to hear the whispered voices through the beating rain outside. The brothers were back. Rusty's soft whinny raised a flurry of shhh's from the two boys as they neared the barn. Henry bit his lip, debating whether or not to crack open the door to see if they had it with them but the clopping of Rusty's hooves and the creaking of wooden wheels revealed they did. Better to keep a distance, he thought.

From behind a stack of hay bales near the entrance, Henry's wiry black body crouched, melting into the darkness as the barn door slid open with a loud creak. The silhouette of two small figures and a horse pulling a wagon showed through the entrance. Then, a light flicked on in the farmhouse across the yard. The boys jerked around.

"Oh no! D-do you think they heard?" stuttered Phil, the smaller one.

Bruce, quite a bit taller, pulled roughly on the horse's rope to urge him along. "Come on. Let's get this thing out of the rain before they find out."

Rusty's hooves echoed on the straw-covered plank floor as the large, covered load rolled into the barn, skimming the top of the doorway as it passed under. Once inside, Bruce dropped the lead rope and helped Phil push the two doors closed.

Darkness filled the barn as the rain pounded on the roof. For nearly a minute Phil, Bruce and Henry stood, listening while rain rattling on the tin roof above.

"Bruce?" whispered Phil.

"Yeah," was the hushed retort.

"Do you think those men followed us?" Phil's voice quivered.

"Well, maybe," said Bruce. "We didn't see them, but they might have. It's too dark in here to do anything."

Footfalls crossed the hay-strewn floor. Then a small clank of metal was followed by a scrape. Light flickered in a lantern as Bruce held it up by his head. Bright blue eyes peered out from beneath tangled curls straggling out from under the dripping leather cap. Henry stared at the loaded buckboard as it sat in the long shadows.

The boys moved Rusty and the wagon around until the load was directly under the middle barn rafter. Phil's wet auburn curls were plastered to his forehead and a mass of freckles were splashed across his nose and cheeks as he struggled to hold Rusty. Bruce grabbed the rope ends dangling from high in the ceiling and knotted them to six sides of the covered load. Then he tied the last, much thicker rope to Rusty's harness. Even though the thick rope still seemed awkward in Bruce's slender hands, he deftly tied two solid knots, leaving the long end dangling down the horse's side.

Circling the load, testing each rope, Bruce gave Phil the thumbs up signal.

"Come on, boy, pull!" Phil pulled at Rusty's bridle rope and the big horse resisted for a moment before stomping forward. When the load creaked and groaned as the ropes tightened around it, Rusty stopped. Bruce slapped the big horse on the rear. The animal whinnied, tossing his head back before leaning forward and pulling. The load, rose off the wagon, dangling in the air for an instant before ascending towards the ceiling rafters. Soon it disappeared into the darkness. Then, with an abrupt thud, the horse halted, dancing in place, his eyes wild.

"Whoa, Rusty," ordered Bruce, yanking on the bridle and stepping in front of the beast.

"How are we going to hold Rusty still to tie this off? Huh, Bruce?" asked Phil.

Henry, watching from his hiding place, abruptly sneezed.

"Is that you, Henry?" demanded Bruce, holding Rusty's head taut.

Henry didn't answer but instead, stepped out beside the bales, his thumbs tucked in the edges of his overalls.

"Come here boy and hold this horse steady and don't you let him move."

Henry stepped up and grasped the bridle straps firmly as Bruce released them. Taller than Bruce, Henry was much thinner. His light brown eyes stood out from his coal black skin like two beacons as he stared straight ahead.

"You better not tell anyone about what we dragged in here, boy," Bruce warned.

"Aw, come on, Bruce. You know he won't tell," insisted Phil. "Shoot, he never talks to anyone. I don't even think he's smart enough to talk."

"No, I think stable boy, here, is smarter than he lets on. But I'm not too worried. I mean, nobody would believe anything a slave boy says anyway."

Bruce looked hard at Henry, who glared back without blinking. Then Bruce turned away to tie the rope from Rusty's harness to the center post. It took almost all of Phil's and Bruce's strength to unhook the taut rope from the horse's bridle. With a snap, the rope pulled tight. They wrapped the end round and round the post, and then finally tied it off with several knots, stacking pitchforks and various tools against the post to hide the rope. Finally, the two boys unhooked the wagon and dragged it into an empty stall.

Rusty seemed content as Henry, who patted him gently on the neck, led the horse to a stall. Minutes later, the big horse stood contentedly chomping on a pail of oats, his dripping harness dangling on a peg outside his stall.

Henry latched the stall door. Sudden shouts from outside brought looks of panic to Bruce and Phil.

"Run and hide!" hissed Bruce as he started for the loft ladder. Phil looked right, then left, undecided as to where to go. Rusty whinnied and stomped in his stall. Henry vanished.

The barn door was flung open and three men in dark, dripping, rain slickers and cowboy hats, tromped in, clutching rifles and lanterns. Following behind was a farmer in denim overalls and a stout woman, huddled together under a single rain slicker.

"You have no right barging in here, deputy," shouted the farmer.

"Shut up, Stromberg," said a tall, hawk-nosed man through clenched teeth. "Those boys of yours are hiding it. I know they are."

"How in the world could two young boys get such a..." started Stromberg, only to be interrupted.

"You're probably in on this thievery as well," the man shouted. He raised his rifle, leveling it at Stromberg. Ice blue, cruel eyes stared at the farmer, daring him to argue. "I have the authority to use whatever means I need to get it back. So if you don't want those boys hurt or thrown in jail, you'd better tell them to come out now."

One of the other two men spotted Phil behind an empty crate and dragged him to the center of the room. Henry crouched lower in the bales.

"I got one of the rats here, Fred. The other one can't be far," he said, throwing the boy to the ground.

"Good job, Jasper." Fred's face lit up with a cruel grimace.

"Oh, Phillip!" shouted the woman. She dashed past her husband to the young boy, sprawled on the ground.

"Stay back out of the way, woman. You don't even belong out here," muttered Fred, pushing her roughly away with the barrel of his rifle. He glared at the farmer. "You can't even control your woman, Stromberg. I guess I shouldn't expect you to control your young'uns any better."

Stromberg lunged at Fred but was knocked to the ground by his swinging rifle stock. He lay quiet, face down, the gash on his head turning the straw red beneath him.

"Dad!" cried Phil, crawling towards his father.

Fred spun around towards Phil, his rifle suddenly exploding at the kneeling boy. A look of confusion filled the boy's eyes as he clutched his stomach, a patch of bright red blossoming over his hand and dripping onto the floor. His mother threw herself between Fred's gun and her wounded son, glaring up at the man's toothy grin.

v

Shorter, heavier Jasper stepped back. His rifle, tucked under his arm, pointed towards the floor. He shook his head, grabbing his hat with his other hand and shaking it violently, spraying water everywhere. "What are you doing, Fred? He's just a boy."

Fred grimaced as he looked at his rifle, caressing the carved stock. "Don't worry. He's only wounded. We'll find out all we need to from the other one. He's got to be hiding around here somewhere." He leveled his rifle as he peered around the barn. Straw trickled from the loft. Fred pointed towards it and pulled the trigger.

"Hey, knock it off, Fred," came the low voice of the third man in the loft. "I think I heard the other one up here. I don't want you hitting me by mistake too.

Fred turned away from Phil and his mother, and clutching his rifle, walked to the loft ladder. "Just try to bring him down alive, Will. I got some talking to do to him."

"Ahhh. There you are." Will's voice was cut short as a figure lunged towards him, tackling him to the floor. Straw rained down on the observers as the two bodies rolled from one end of the loft to the other. It was impossible to tell them apart from below. Henry watched as they bumped up against the loft's wooden railing and post. Fred raised his rifle several times towards the bodies but lowered it each time. Then, with a crack, the railing splintered and broke apart. Bruce and Will came crashing down through the hole, landing with a thud on the wooden floor. Will rolled off Bruce's still body.

"Well, that's just fine!" raged Fred, stomping past Will, who sat clutching his ankle and nudging Bruce with his foot. He poked the barrel of his rifle at Bruce's prone body. There was no response.

"Oh, I don't think he's dead, Fred. He just passed out," said Will.

Fred kicked a bundle of straw towards Will. "Don't matter. Can't tell us a thing now. We'll have to come back later. But we'll get it out of one of them. I'll make 'em tell us where they hid it." He stomped around the post where the boys had tied the rope, knocking over a stool and a few of the tools leaning up against it. "It ain't here. Come on boys. We're wasting our time," Fred growled. He whipped his still dripping hat off his head and slapped it on his knee, water flying everywhere, before jamming it back onto his head.

Henry noticed that Stromberg was sitting up now, holding his head, blood running down his arm. Stromberg glared up at Fred. "Get out! You and your men get off my place."

Fred rested the barrel of his rifle on Bruce's prone body. "We'll be back. If you want to save those boys of yours, you'd better get them to confess where they hid it. If they won't tell, we'll just have to convince your wife or you to spill the beans."

"Get out! Get off my property. NOW!" yelled Stromberg in a voice so furious it made his wife gasp.

"Stupid farmer!" Fred muttered, stomping out, Will and Jasper close behind.

Stromberg tried to calm his weeping wife as they huddled beside their two sons. Henry couldn't understand what they said when they talked in German, but by the tone of their voices, he knew they were arguing. The farmer's wife kept motioning towards the door and Stromberg repeatedly threw up his hands in a look of defeat, shaking his head. They finally grew silent as they gazed at the still bodies of the boys. Slowly, they gathered them up, and dousing the lanterns in the barn, left, closing the doors behind them. Henry watched through the window as they carried Phil and Bruce to the farmhouse. In the silence of the barn, Henry stepped out and peered up into the dark rafters. It would be safe up there.

Back in the stall on the soft pile of straw that was his bed, he realized how tired he was. But first, he had to brush down Rusty.

****

The next morning, Stromberg came out to the barn earlier than usual. Henry had just finished feeding the livestock when he heard the barn door slide open.

"Dead. They're both dead. Do you hear me, Henry?" The bitter softness of Stromberg's voice frightened Henry.

His eyes widened as he vigorously shook his head. The boys are dead?

"The missus is not herself and I...well, I don't know what to do. Our sons were everything. We are going to go away for a while. Those men will be back but they won't find us here. You best be gone too. Here's the back pay I owe you." He grabbed Henry's hand and put a handful of coins in it, closing his long slender fingers gently around them. "Finish up your chores for today then I'll have to let you know when we come back. When we come back..." he repeated, his voice trailing off. Unblinking, Stromberg walked calmly out of the barn and back to the farmhouse.

Henry stared down at the money in his hands, but it was all a blur. Both boys are dead. How could they both be dead? Phil probably bled to death but Bruce didn't fall that far from the loft. How could he have died too? Those men would be back to question him if they found out he worked there. He couldn't stay. He'd have to find another job somewhere else.

He propped his pitchfork against the rope-wound post, then retrieved his blanket bundle. Opening it up, he laid aside the faded tin-type photo of his mother and baby sister, the new, white cloth shirt that had been given to him,

viii

an old rusty screwdriver and hammer, the tarnished pocket watch that had belonged to his grandfather and the Bible. He picked up the heavy book and opened it. He leafed through it, until he came upon two neatly folded blank pieces of paper. These had been saved for something special or an emergency. This was an emergency. He pulled a pencil stub from the pocket of his overalls and with his pearl handled pocketknife, whittled the end to a writable point.

Henry unfolded one of the sheets and wrote:

August 3, 1912

Dear Mr. Whitehead,
I hope you won't be mad when you find out about Phil and Bruce hiding No. 22 last night. They done it so it wouldn't get burnt up with the other things those men took from you and were killed for their trouble. I hear people say you lost that trial because you was a German person and people are afraid of you. It's not fair. I know where No. 22 is because I watched the boys hide it. It is safe and I won't tell no one. I'm really going to miss working at your shop but I have to go away for a while.
Your friend,
Henry Andrew Jackson

He read it twice, and then folded it carefully in half, intending on dropping it off at Mr. Whitehead's house before he left town. But as he held the letter in his hand, there was a commotion out in the yard. He stuffed it back into the Bible, threw the book and his other possessions onto the blanket and grabbed up the corners. With the bundle clutched tightly to his chest, he dashed behind two large barrels, and then wove through the maze of hay bales until he could see the half-open barn door.

"The old man is either in the barn or at the house. I'll take the house, you search the barn," came the familiar voice from the night before.

The barn door squeaked loudly as it slid open. Will, the man who fought with Bruce in the loft, stood for an instant with the rifle cradled in his arms, squinting into the gloomy barn. He sauntered over to the loft ladder and began climbing it. Suddenly, the hawk-faced man's voice came from the house's front porch, "You can't hide from me, Stromberg. Where the hell are you?"

Henry shuddered then slipped quietly past the corner bale, out the door into the farm yard, just as the man crashed in through the front door of the house. Henry dashed towards the tall maples lining the lane, clutching his bundle to his chest. Afraid to look back, his own heart beat so loudly, he was sure they would hear it. Behind a sturdy tree trunk, he squatted, his back against it, trying to catch his breath. Things were quiet. Then shouts rang out and a woman's scream was followed by two gun shots. Henry jerked his head around staring at the house. A gust of wind blew Stromberg's straw hat that he always wore across the yard. Henry knew he had to keep the secret. He glanced back once, at the barn with its brightly colored rooster sitting quietly atop, its mouth open as if in a silent scream, and then made his way down the lane. Away.

Chapter One

Discovery

My fifth rejection slip lay open beside the ripped envelope on the passenger's seat as if to shout, "loser!" Rain pounded the windshield as I pulled up in front of Grandma D's house, put the car in park and turned off the lights. *Nothing seems to be going right today. First the rejection slip, then my tail light goes out and now this deluge.*

I stomped up the sagging steps onto the front porch of the old, two-story, yellow house, scraping my muddy shoes on the outdoor mat. As I shook the water off of my umbrella, Grandma opened the door. "Lorie! Come in out of this nasty weather! My, it's so dark for being midmorning." Her wispy white hair, unruly as always, almost resembled a nervous creature perched on her nodding head. I sighed and smiled. *Things never change. Kudos to you, Mom, for suggesting this stop on my way back down to Illinois.* Grandma gave me a big hug. "So good to see you, child. I've been waiting for you since your mother called saying you were coming." I hung my jacket and dripping umbrella on the coat tree in the entrance before slipping out of my muddy shoes.

The living room, a welcome oasis with its faded, yellow wallpaper and the ornate decorations in the wood around the windows and doorways seemed to transport me back to a simpler time, a peaceful time without heavy traffic and TV and ringing phones.

"You seem troubled," Grandma said. "Tell me what's wrong while I put on the kettle. You'll have a nice cup of tea with me, won't you?" She stepped ahead of me through the dining room and into the kitchen.

"Yes, I'd love one," I replied. "You wouldn't believe it, but I just got another rejection slip on that covered bridge article I sent off. I know it's because I'm female. If I'd been a guy, they would have had no trouble accepting my article. Nobody wants any of the stuff I write. It's just not fair."

"Don't worry." She shook her head. "Someone will if you're persistent. Don't give up, child. Never give up. You are a fine writer. You just need to find the right story, or maybe the right story needs to find you."

"I just don't know. It seems all anyone wants to read about these days is the war in Vietnam or the Hollywood scene. I want something different. You know, something that should be told that hasn't been.".

"Oh, there's the kettle. Go relax in the library and pick out a nice book and I'll bring in the tea."

I browsed through the built-in bookshelves in the library, just off the living room, while the tick-tick of the corner mantel clock echoed. *Shakespeare, Walt Whitman, Lincoln, Chaucer, Will Rogers. Nothing really appeals to me.* I sighed and plopped down on the leather window-seat, overlooking the front yard and the street. *I really love this old house: its musty scent, tall ceilings, dark polished wood furniture, and silence.*

Grandma slowly approached with two mugs of steaming tea. I stood up and in two steps met her at the room's archway. "Here, let me hold those while you get situated in your chair," I insisted, taking them both. She sat in the rocker and spread a bright blue and green, crocheted comforter over her knees. I handed her a mug. "Do you need anything else? TV or something to read?"

"No, thank you, dear. I'll just rest my eyes for a spell. Couldn't sleep well last night."

2

As I sat back in the window-seat, I glanced up at the corner clock's bold face: 11:14. The rain tapped against the window, making a blur of the street and the passing car lights. The morning was nearly gone and, with a yawn, I contemplated simply curling up and taking a nap. Grandmother dozed in the adjoining living room in her rocker, her tea mug tucked into her lap.

The quarter-hour BONG of the old clock startled me. I loved the graceful swirls of its mahogany case that framed the bold face and ran the entire length and width of the library. The clock sat right in the corner with bookcases rising to the ceiling on either side. *It's a wonder that old clock still works after all these years.*

The glass-doored book cases were packed with leather-bound volumes, some dating back to the Civil War. As I studied the intricate carving of the pillars on either side of the clock-face itself and the curlicues on the small tower that rose behind it, something light brown protruded from behind the face. Maybe it's the key, I thought, pulling a rickety folding chair from the card table in the middle of the room, over to the corner. In my sock feet, I stepped cautiously onto it. However, even with my 5'2" frame fully extended, my head only reached the bottom edge of the corner tower. Unable to see behind it, I reached up and over the scalloped wooden edges around the face and along the metal backing into the empty space in the corner, holding my breath and hoping not to disturb an unsuspecting spider. Kittens of dust floated up as I moved about, finally closing my fingers around something flat and stiff. I coughed as I pulled out a rectangular booklet from behind the clock, creating a mini-dust storm. I sneezed, trying to stifle the sound so as not to awake Grandma. A tear crept down my cheek, which I attempted to brush away with my sleeve. I stepped down from the chair and used both hands to lay a grimy 6" x 9" tablet on the card table. Gently wiping the cover with a folded Kleenex from my jeans pocket, I revealed "William J. Meyer, 13 November, 1889," in flowing letters on the cover.

3

Seated at the wobbly card table, I opened the frail tablet that was bound at the top. Life-like pencil drawings of animals, men working, and children playing along with a variety of ornate woodworking patterns leapt off the pages. The highly detailed drawings were each captioned with flowing, handwritten script, complete with dates. Several blank pages separated the drawings from ten or fifteen pages of precise writing filling the remainder of the notebook. Unable to read the flowery German script like I'd only previously seen in books, I carefully turned each page using both hands. At one point, I noticed an underlined passage and squinting, deciphered the name "Gustave Weisskopf." I whispered the name several times while leafing through the remaining pages. At the back of the tablet was a folded newspaper clipping, which had stuck itself onto the inside cover. Crisp as a pressed fall leaf, the paper tore slightly as I pried it loose, leaving a lighter imprint in the stiff cardboard backing. Slowly, I unfolded the article: "Inventors in Partnership to Solve Problem of Aerial Navigation," which had been clipped from an August 19, 1901 New York Herald.

"What have you got there?" Grandma's voice surprised me.

"Oh, I didn't know you were awake. Did you know there was a notebook hidden behind this clock?"

"Bring it here, child. Let me see."

Although Grandma was nearly blind, I took the tablet over to her.

"Wasn't William J. Meyer your father?" I asked, pointing to the cover.

"Why, yes. Is that his sketchbook? I wondered what had happened to that. You said you found it behind the clock? I think your Aunt Jean hid it there when she was just a girl. Father was a fine artist, wasn't he?" She smiled and took a sip of her tea.

4

"These drawings are incredible!" I exclaimed. "How old was he in 1889? That's the date on the cover."

"Let me see." She tapped her hand lightly on her forehead. "That would have made him 18 years old. He had just come over on a boat from Germany and was trying to find work as a carpenter. Even though he spent a short time in New York City, he didn't like living in a big city. I'm not quite sure why he settled here in Michigan, but I think it has something to do with meeting my mother. Both my sister and I were born right here in Centreville."

"Do you know anything about this 1901 newspaper article that was tucked in the back?" I asked, returning the booklet to the card table. I carefully unfolded the clipping and spread it out.

"Read it aloud, child, and we'll see," replied Grandma with a slight wave of her hand.

I read the bold heading:

"INVENTORS IN PARTNERSHIP TO SOLVE PROBLEM OF AERIAL NAVIGATION. Gustave Whitehead Travels Half a Mile in Flying Machine Operated by a new Acetylene Chemical Pressure, Lessening Motor Power Weight Seventy-Five Per Cent."

I paused before continuing with the article:

"BRIDGEPORT, Conn., Sunday. With the purpose in view of perfecting a flying machine that will solve the problem of aerial navigation to the point of commercial success, Gustave Whitehead, of this city, and W.D. Custead, of Waco, Texas, have formed a partnership. Both men are inventors. Mr. Whitehead last Tuesday night, with two assistants, took his machine to a long field back of Fairfield and the inventor, for the first time flew in his machine for half a mile. It worked perfectly, and the operator found no difficulty in handling it. Mr. Whitehead's machine is equipped with two engines, one

5

to propel it on the ground, on wheels, and the other to make the wings or propellers work."

I read the rest of the article dealing mostly with Whitehead's unique motor used in the flight. Mr. Custead and his airships were mentioned near the end of the article with a hint of a combined machine to come:

"The good points of both inventors' flying machines will be included in the new machine and this combination, with the new acetylene chemical pressure generator, it is believed, will produce the desired results in the way of a flying machine."

I shook my head in amazement. "Wow. I'll bet that was some machine they had. Have you ever heard of such a thing?"

"No, dear. You shouldn't worry your pretty little head about such things. Better to leave it to college professors and historians. But if Roy were here, he probably would know, having been so interested in aviation. He was the best pilot..." Her voice faded away as she closed her eyes.

The ticking of the clock dominated the silent room. I gently removed the tea mug from her lap and pulled the comforter up around her.

Back at the card table, I reread the article, and then opened the tablet to the page containing the underlined script. *Gustave is not such a common name. Weisskopf. Whitehead. But of course! 'Weisskopf' literally translates to 'White head.' It must be the same guy as in the article. William Meyer must have known this Whitehead fellow. I wish I could translate the rest of this.*

Refolding it, I carefully placed it back in the tablet where it had been. Behind Grandma, above the couch, I glimpsed a pair of wings in a large dusty frame, which was

6

actually a collection of photos and a newspaper article of the Wright Brothers' first flight. The bold print at the top read:

"THE ORIGINAL WRIGHT BROTHERS AEROPLANE, THE WORLD'S FIRST POWER-DRIVEN, HEAVIER-THAN-AIR MACHINE IN WHICH MAN MADE FREE, CONTROLLED, AND SUSTAINED FLIGHT, INVENTED AND BUILT BY WILBUR AND ORVILLE WRIGHT; FLOWN BY THEM AT KITTY HAWK, NORTH CAROLINA, DECEMBER 17, 1903.

BY ORIGINAL SCIENTIFIC RESEARCH THE WRIGHT BROTHERS DISCOVERED THE PRINCIPLES OF HUMAN FLIGHT AS INVENTORS, BUILDERS, AND FLYERS THEY FURTHER DEVELOPED THE AEROPLANE, TAUGHT MAN TO FLY, AND OPENED THE ERA OF AVIATION."

The words at the bottom right corner read, "By the Smithsonian National Air and Space Museum."

I ran my fingers over the December 17, 1903 date. A chill ran up my spine as I backed away from the couch. *How can that be? Someone has made a mistake. The flight in the article is dated 1901, a whole two years before the Wright Brothers' flight. Just who is this Gustave Whitehead and why haven't I ever heard of him? Boy, what an article this will make!*

Chapter Two

Andy

I closed the car door, not bothering to lock it, and jogged through the sprawling college parking lot to the sidewalk. The Illinois morning sun glistened off the damp grass as I gazed up at the three-story brick building erected in 1860 called Old Main, which had been the main campus in earlier days. *Even after spending four years here getting my degree, I never tire of this charming structure, with its castle-like towers at each end.* Vines crept up its sides nearly obscuring the faded beige brick walls. I paused in front of the quaint old building, and then with a sigh, rounded the corner. The Old Main Clock tower, situated majestically above the rest, showed I had only two minutes to reach my desk. A group of contemporary tinted-windowed buildings filled the rest of the main campus, reminding me of invading aliens from some space movie. Heading towards the two-story, pyramid-shaped Library at the far end of the campus, I picked up my pace.

When my hand touched the front door handle, a voice, seemingly from nowhere, made me jump.

"Allow me."

My friend, Ben, grinned down at me as he held open the door.

"Oh! I didn't see you sneak up," I exclaimed, walking into the Library ahead of him. "Did you have a good weekend?"

Ben Spinelli was probably over 6' and pencil thin. His free hand was jammed into the pocket of his navy blue slacks as he followed me inside. The blue-gray sweater vest over a white shirt with a skinny dark tie was more

8

conservative than any of the students browsing the stacks. Black-rimmed glasses slid down his long, curved nose as he walked. He unconsciously pushed them up every few steps. Although Ben was no Tom Cruise, he had a certain boyish appeal with that mass of curly black hair and happy-go-lucky grin. "Yeah, it was OK. How was your visit with your Grandmother in Michigan?"

"She's doing fine but it rained almost the entire weekend. I just sat in the library and looked at old books. You would have loved the old hymnals, all from different churches, that she has collected over the years. I never knew she even went to church," I replied with a chuckle.

Ben elbowed me in the side as their supervisor walked rapidly towards us. Willowy Mrs. Comstock, peering over the top of her horn-rimmed reading glasses, glared at us and then looked up at the clock. I had barely plopped my purse onto the front desk when the big hand jerked onto the 12. Mrs. Comstock cleared her throat as she swished past into her office, shutting the door firmly. Ben rolled his eyes and mouthed a quick "Bye" before hurrying off upstairs.

Before I uncovered my typewriter, I stashed a manila envelope, which I'd tucked inside my raincoat, down under my desk. *How am I going to get into that card catalogue to look up Gustave Whitehead without raising suspicion? I have to cover the front desk and process new books all the time, and never get into the stacks unless a student requests something.* As I hung up my raincoat on the row of pegs by Mrs. Comstock's office, I glimpsed Ben behind the 2nd floor railing, wheeling out a cart full of books to put away.

I flipped on the typewriter's power switch and inserted a blank card-sized slip of paper, then took down the first new book on the pile. I opened its cover, just in case nosy Mrs. Comstock didn't think I was doing something "work related." Then I typed a message to Ben: "Would you look up information on "Gustave Whitehead" or "Gustave

9

Weisskopf" in the card catalogue? Meet me at the student union for lunch and I'll explain."

****

The morning crept by in spite of all the work piled before me. Around 10:30, Mrs. Comstock strode past and out the front door with her umbrella in hand. I stood, keeping my eye on the entrance in case she suddenly returned. After a minute, it was obvious she wasn't coming back right away, so I grabbed the note to Ben and sauntered out into the middle of the library. Scanning both floors, I finally spotted his cart at the far corner on the almost empty 2nd floor. *It shouldn't take more than a minute to deliver the note.*

When I stepped onto the upper landing, Ben came around a corner almost colliding with me, carrying an oversized volume with both hands.

"What are you doing up here?" he whispered, looking around for the ever-watchful Mrs. Comstock.

I thrust the note at him. "If you get a chance, would you look this name up for me? I gotta get back before you-know-who returns and finds the front desk empty."

Ben, paper in hand, watched as I turned and fled down the stairs. Just as I slid back in my desk chair, Mrs. Comstock, umbrella tucked under her arm, stepped back through the front door and glared at the front desk.

She approached me and shook her head. Her loud raspy whisper carried all through the library. "If you're going to take a break, you must make it snappy. No lingering. Understand? Now make a mimeograph of this memo for the employees and run me off ten copies."

With that, she slapped a handwritten note on my desk, and then hurried into her office. In three strides, she

10

was back behind the front desk. I sighed and dragged a blank sheet out of the packet in the bottom drawer of my desk. *I hate typing mimeographs. I can never not make a mistake, and then my hands get all purple from scraping the inky type off with a razorblade.* I grabbed a couple of tissues for my undoubtedly, soon-to-be stained fingers.

It was a relief when the clock finally struck 12:30. Sharon, on time as usual, stepped up to the front desk to cover during the lunch break. Grabbing raincoat and the manila envelope, I walked out the front door into the bright sunlight, pausing only a moment to soak in the fresh moist air. Ben appeared at my side and we walked together to the Student Union.

Jabbering students and teachers crowded the cafeteria. We ended up standing in a line snaking back along the wall from the counter. By 12:50, most of the people had straggled out for 1:00 classes and by 12:55, it was almost deserted. By then, Ben and I had filled our trays and taken them to a booth by the window.

I set down my tray, then called to one of the teachers who sat a few table away.

"Herr Meinz!"

"Lorie, Ben," he acknowledged. "It's a beautiful day out there. So how are the books treating you at the library?"

Herr Meinz had been one of my oldest and dearest friends from college. We had met my first day on campus over four years ago and I'd worked as his assistant in the German department that first semester. He was Aryan-handsome with those deep-blue eyes, firm, straight nose, and strawberry blond hair.

"Oh, the books love us. But I'm not so sure about Mrs. Comstock," I replied.

11

I pulled Great-grandfather's frail tablet from the envelope and handed it to the professor.

"What do we have here?" he asked, opening it and perusing the delicate sheets.

"Would you be able to do me a big favor? This is my great-grandfather's diary from 1889. I can't make out much of this German script. Could you do a translation for me, if you have the time?"

"This looks fascinating. I can see how you would have trouble with this, though. Sure. But I won't be able to get it back to you right away."

"Oh, anytime would be great. Thanks."

He gave me a wink and walked away, glancing down at the sheets and nearly colliding with a group of students coming into the Union.

Ben had been sitting at the booth stuffing french-fries into his mouth. He leaned across the table closer when I finally sat down. "OK, the suspense is killing me. What's going on here? What's all this Whitehead, Weisskopf stuff about?"

I leaned across the table and in between bites of hamburger, told him about the discovery of the journal, the newspaper articles and the Wright Brothers plaque hanging above Grandmother's couch. He sat quietly, sipping his milkshake, listening to me go on about how I just had to find out about this man and his early flights and what a perfect article it would make to launch my writing career.

Then I remembered the phone call I'd wanted to make during lunch. Excusing myself, I headed for the phone booth near the entrance, stepped inside and pulled shut the accordion door.

The quarters, dimes and nickels, clinked onto the stainless steel ledge under the phone as I emptied my coin purse, ready to plug them in when the operator told me how much. Then, I dialed the number, tapping the edge of the phone ledge with a pencil as the phone rang four times. After depositing the proper change, a woman's voice answered. I asked to talk to Brad Peters, assistant editor at a magazine called History's Mysteries.

"One moment, please," replied the operator.

"Brad Peters here."

"Oh, Mr. Peters, this is Lorie Drucker. I wrote that article about hang-gliders a year or so ago and you told me if I came up with a great idea, you'd help me sell it to your boss. Well, boy, do I have one!"

Ten minutes later, I had elicited a promise from him to show my finished article to his boss, with the understanding that he couldn't guarantee a sale. He warned me I'd have to have solid proof that this guy flew or the article would go directly into the trash. And he wanted it on his desk no later than April 10th, just two weeks after Easter Sunday. *This is the chance I've waited and hoped for!*

The library was quiet all afternoon until about 3:00 when most of the classes let out and students flocked in, gathered in groups, murmuring and whispering among themselves, ignoring the angry looks from Mrs. Comstock, who insisted on a quiet library. I glanced at the clock as a young colored student in an old tattered military jacket walked up to the front desk and dropped an army-green backpack on the floor beside him.

"Do you need some help?" I asked.

"Yes ma'am. Where could I find your periodicals? This is my first time in your library and I'm kind of lost," he said with a shy smile.

13

"Oh, the magazines are upstairs at the back on the right side," I pointed. "The stairs are right back there."

"Thanks." He slung his pack over one shoulder and walked away.

A little more than an hour later, I sat outside on the library steps, waiting for Ben, who finally burst through the door.

"Sorry I'm late. Had to finish filing some last minute periodicals from the dragon lady," he explained.

"That's OK. Did you come up with anything on Whitehead?"

"Well, you won't believe what happened. Come on. We can grab a Coke at the Union. I don't like hanging around here when I don't have to."

We walked back towards the Union, dodging bicycles and jogging students. A slight breeze rustled the leaves of the ancient oaks surrounding Old Main. The clouded sky looked like it might rain. I zipped up my raincoat, listening intently to Ben.

"This colored guy, Andy, came up to me while I was putting away magazines and asked for help. Did you notice him come in with that pack slung over his back?" I nodded. "He seemed like a real nice guy. You'll never guess what he was looking for," declared Ben.

I gave him that I'm-in-no-mood-for-guessing-games-look, so he picked up the pace and continued, walking faster. I almost had to jog to keep up with him. "Yeah, he came to the front desk looking for magazines."

"Well, he wanted to find information on one Gustave Whitehead. I couldn't believe my ears. But he was the

14

customer, right? So, I looked the name up and found one article written by Gustave Whitehead in an April, 1902 copy of The American Inventor, which described two, not one, but two flights he made in January, that same year. Wow, was I surprised. Well, Andy copied down most of the article and seemed really excited. I don't know what he was going to do with it, but he thanked me profusely."

I can't believe what he'd said! "There is an article in The American Inventor? Oh, I'd sure like to talk to Andy. If he comes in again and I don't notice him, give me the high sign."

Only a few couples and teachers lingered at the Union over Styrofoam coffee cups. Ben and I settled in our favorite window booth with Cokes.

"There's more," Ben said, unfolding a small square of paper from his pocket. He looked at it as he said, "I found out there was a book published about Gustave Whitehead called, Lost Flights of Gustave Whitehead, by Stella Randolph."

I stared down at the paper, and then looked back at Ben. "Well, don't keep me in suspense. Do we have a copy of it?"

"'Fraid not," he replied, shaking his head. "But there is a copy at the Chicago Public Library, so I took the liberty of ordering it, under Andy's name, of course. It should be here in two days."

"Oh Ben, you're the greatest!" I exclaimed. "Two days. I don't know if I can wait that long."

Ben slid out of the booth and snatched his Coke off the table. "Listen, I've got to get home. See you tomorrow, Lorie."

I sighed as Ben wove his way through the jumble of tables and chairs to the glass doors. *He is such a nice guy. It's cute that he has a crush on me but I have to be careful not to lead him into believing I'm really interested in him. Our friendship is too important.*

As I stared out the window at the massive music building across the street, students trickled out through a side door into the alley. *Choir must be out. It always gets out late on Mondays.* Clumps of students dispersed in various directions. A single colored boy in a baseball cap, with an army backpack slung over one shoulder, walked towards a pale blue VW Bug parked right in front of the Union. *Why, that looks like Andy.* I squinted, trying to see the face beneath the hat. *That has to be Andy, especially with that backpack.* I wanted to yell "Stop!" but knew he couldn't hear me inside the Union, so I grabbed up my purse and ran out.

But by the time I reached the sidewalk, he had pulled the Bug out of the space and zipped past me towards town. As he coasted to a halt before the Stop sign, the bumper sticker, "MY OTHER CAR IS A PORSCHE" made me smile. *Tomorrow I'll find that car.*

Chapter Three

The Call

The next morning, I was busy typing and suddenly Mrs. Comstock crept up behind me and said in a loud whisper, "There is a student waiting."

"Yes Ma'am." I stood up and turned towards the front desk, catching Mrs. Comstock, out of the corner of my eye, snatching the stapler and hurrying back to her office.

When I saw who was at the front desk, I blurted, much too loudly, "You're back!"

Andy, his army-green pack slung over one shoulder, looked around to see if I was talking to someone else. Then he looked back with a crooked smile. "Are you talking to me?"

"Well, er, uh, yes," I stammered.

"You might have me confused with one of the other colored kids on campus. You know what they say," he grinned, "we all look alike."

I emphatically shook my head. "No! No, you don't all look alike and yes, I was looking for you." Then leaning over the desk, I said in a hushed voice, "You were looking for information about Gustave Whitehead, weren't you?"

He leaned in and whispered, "Yes. Am I not allowed to do that?"

17

"Of course you are," I said. "I must talk to you about Whitehead and that article you found yesterday. Can you meet me at the Union around 12:45 today?"

"I suppose so," he said. "Are you sure you want to be seen with me? You know, people will talk."

I snapped back, "Yes, I'm sure. It doesn't bother me one bit." *Well, it shouldn't.*

"Now, where might I find some information about the Wright Brothers' first flight?" he asked, as I heard Mrs. Comstock's door latch behind me. I looked around as she laid the stapler back on my desk and glared at me. I glanced back at Andy, trying hard not to roll my eyes.

"You will find it over there in our history section." I pointed out the area.

"Thank you, Ma'am." With a nod, he hitched up his tattered backpack and walked away.

I whispered after him, "And my name is Lorie, not Ma'am."

I wasn't sure if he heard as he walked away. Rolling a new book card into my typewriter, I wondered if Andy was serious or just teasing me. *He certainly seems touchy about being a negro. But, that won't stop me from finding out why he is interested in Gustave Whitehead and the Wright Brothers.*

Ben and I carried our lunch trays to our favorite booth, sliding in opposite each other. "Do you think he'll show up?" I wondered out loud. "I sure hope so."

No sooner had I said it when Andy appeared at the booth with a steaming cup of coffee. He set it down, shrugged out of his pack, and pulled up a chair to the end of the table.

"Why do you carry that old thing," asked Ben, nodding at the threadbare, green knapsack on the floor by Andy's chair. "I've never seen any other students with them. Don't you have a locker?"

"No, there weren't any left, or at least that's what they told me," he said, staring at Ben's food instead of Ben. "Besides, I don't have to waste time between classes going to a locker because I can carry everything with me in there. It sure beats hauling armfuls of books and dropping stuff constantly." He laid one hand on it. "This was my dad's old army pack and I'm proud to use it."

"So, Andy," I said, leaning towards him. "Why are you so interested in Gustave Whitehead?"

"Boy, you don't waste any time, do you? Well," he paused, taking a sip of his coffee. "I found an old letter at my Aunt's house in our family Bible at Christmas this year. My Great-Uncle Henry wrote it when he was a kid about how he used to work for someone named Gustave Whitehead. I was curious about it, seeing how Uncle really seemed to admire this Whitehead guy. He mentioned something about an airplane Whitehead built called 'Number 22' and how he saw someone hide it." He looked me straight in the eye. "So how do you know about Whitehead? It's been really difficult finding stuff about him."

I told him about my discovery at Grandmother's house: the 1901 article, the journal and the Wright Brothers' plaque of their 1903 first flight. Andy, leaning over the table, seemed totally enthralled. But when I finished, and glanced over at Ben, he was more interested in a group of girls pointing to our table and giggling. Two couples at a table nearby picked up their trays and moved to a table farther away, and the three teachers who sat in the booth behind them hurriedly drained their coffee cups and left.

"What's going on?" I asked Ben.

He shrugged his shoulders, staring at his Coke cup.

"I'll tell you what's going on." Andy crushed his Styrofoam cup with one hand. "They don't like me sitting here talking to white folks. As long as I'm sitting alone or with 'my kind' it's OK, but I'm not good enough to talk to you. Maybe I'd better leave." His chair screeched on the floor as he stood.

"No! That's ridiculous," I insisted, grabbing his jacket sleeve as if to stop him from leaving.

At that moment, two tall boys strode by our booth, laughing and giving Andy the thumbs up sign. One of them kicked his pack over as he walked by, while the other nudged his friend in the ribs with his elbow. "Hey, I wonder if it is true that once you've had black you won't ever go back!"

My face felt flushed as I opened her mouth to respond. But nothing came out. I snatched up the napkin from the table and loudly blew my nose. Andy retrieved his pack and sat back down.

Ben nodded towards the two guys. "Aw, don't let them get to you, Lorie. They're not worth the trouble."

Andy shook his head and squeezed his crumpled cup tighter. "Listen, I'm sorry. I'd better be going. Maybe we can talk later." Then he rose, grabbed his pack and in four long strides, was out of the room.

****

Back in the library, words like bigotry, narrow-mindedness, prejudice, racist, discrimination and chauvinist pig floated in my mind as I worked that afternoon. *If only I could have thought of them when those two guys*

20

confronted us earlier. It's hard to believe other people can be so nasty just because Andy is colored.

I have to find out more about his Uncle Henry's letter. However, after that little episode in the Union, I doubt I'll ever see Andy again. But, his Uncle Henry had actually worked for Gustave Whitehead!

There must be a way to contact Andy. I gathered up a stack of magazines a student had dropped on the front desk. An old issue of "Life" with the Wright Brother's Kitty Hawk display in the Smithsonian Museum splashed on the cover caught my attention. *That's it! I'll call someone at the Museum. Surely they'll know all about Whitehead and his flights.* I hurriedly put the other magazines on their appropriate racks and nearly ran back to my desk, clutching that copy of Life.

After skimming the article, I laid the magazine aside and grabbed a Washington DC phone directory. The Smithsonian listing had a long list of names and numbers. *But which one should I call?* I ran my finger down the list, stopping on the name Geoffrey Watson. *My brother had brought a cute friend home from college years ago named Geoffrey Watson. He'd been a history major. Could he be the same one?*

Hearing Mrs. Comstock's office door open behind me, I stuffed in a piece of paper to mark my place and closed the book. I moved things around as if to organize my desk. Mrs. Comstock was watching me but I pretended not to notice her.

"Did you finish processing that book on the Presidents?" she asked.

I straightened and turned to face her. "Oh yes Ma'am. I didn't know you were standing there."

"Very well, I'll take it now." She thrust out her hand.

From the heap of books on the corner of my desk, I expertly snatched the heavy book from the middle of the stack, barely moving the rest of the pile.

A glance at the clock and a quick time-change calculation told me it was too late in the day to call the Museum, so I scribbled down the number and vowed to try first thing in the morning.

****

At 8:00 a.m. the next day, after gulping the last of my orange juice, I dialed the Museum number. It rang seven times before someone finally picked it up.

"Hello!" answered a nasally female voice. As an afterthought she added, "Smithsonian Museum, may I help you?"

"Would Geoffrey Watson be there?" I asked.

"I'll have to go check if he's in yet. Please hold."

The phone went dead. I paced a few steps over and a few steps back, wishing I'd bought one of those extra-long phone cords. Three minutes later, sure they'd forgotten me, I decided to hang up and call back later, when the line clicked.

"Hello?" I stared at the telephone wall unit with its lighted numbered dial.

"Yes, yes, who is this?" said a male voice.

"Geoffrey Watson?"

"Speaking," he replied brusquely.

"My name is Lorie Drucker and I'm calling from Illinois. Are you, by chance the same Geoffrey Watson who'd visited us from Culver, in Michigan with my brother, Jon, seven years ago?"

He laughed. "Oh, you were his gawky teenage sister who followed us everywhere." Without giving me a chance to answer, he launched into a rehashing of his trip to our house, laughing and joking about his earlier school years. I looked at the clock and as the big hand crept towards the 3, decided I needed to cut this short. I didn't want to be late for work.

"Listen," I interrupted, "I called to find out some information about a person connected with early motorized flight. Can you help me?"

"I'm proud to say we have the largest collection of Wright Brothers memorabilia in the United States. What would you like to know about them?"

"No, I need to know about someone named Gustave Whitehead of Bridgeport, Connecticut, who actually flew two years before the Wrights. Do you know something about him?" I asked.

"Weisskopf? Uh, er, Gustave Whitehead? I, uh, listen, my boss just walked in. Uh, it's been nice talking to you, but I gotta go. Give my best to your brother." Click.

He hung up. *He actually hung up. But why? It's odd that he said the name "Weisskopf" first. He must have known something about him to have known that. Maybe his boss really did walk in and give him the evil eye. I'll have to wait and call him again during my lunch break, from the payphone at the Union.* I grabbed a hand full of change before leaving the house.

****

23

The darkness outside seemed eerie at 10:30 in the morning. I was glad to be inside the library that nasty March day. Freezing rain pinged against the large windows. Streetlights shone through the sleet as they beamed from their turn-of-the-century lampposts around the campus. Tall, gnarled oaks lining the sidewalks whipped in the wind.

Morning slipped by quicker than usual as inclement weather tended to bring more students into the library. I was kept busy at the front desk stamping books, giving directions, and answering a myriad of questions. I stared at the large stack of new books that had magically appeared next to the typewriter overnight. *I wonder how I'll ever get it all finished.*

As Ben dashed by, leading a couple of students towards the Current Magazines rack he winked at me. For one brief moment, when the crowds disappeared, he slipped up to the desk and whispered, "Hey, the dragon lady wants me to stay while you go to lunch today, so I'll have to catch you later, after work." Then he hurried away, a line forming behind him.

I was still at the front desk five minutes past my normal lunch break when my boss approached.

Mrs. Comstock edged in and stamped a book for a waiting student. "Lorie, go on to lunch. I'll cover the desk until Ben is freed up. But be back on time."

I smiled and muttered a thank you. *She's human after all!* Shrugging into my rain coat and flipping up the hood, I clutched my purse to my side before stepping out into the pouring rain. The wind tore at my hood as I splashed down the steps toward the Student Union. As they hurried by, students struggled against the wind gusts to keep their umbrellas from turning wrong side out. *I'm glad I left mine in the car today.*

My growling stomach reminded me to get something to eat before trying to call Geoffrey Watson. So, with a couple of Twinkies in one hand and cocoa in the other, I headed for the large phone booth outside the cafeteria, in the lobby of the Union. Kicking the door open, I squeezed into the tiny cubicle and set my food carefully on the small ledge in front of the phone. I sat on the edge of the black stationary stool and dug out a handful of change, along with the scrap of paper with Geoffrey's number.

This time, I got through to him with no waiting. However, when he realized it was me, his tone became hushed and cautious.

"Listen, I can't talk about that guy right now. How about if I call you back later, after I get off work. Give me your number and I'll call you this evening," he said in a low voice.

I gave him my home phone number then asked, "Hey, what is it about Gustave Whitehead anyway?"

His reply was sharp and angry. "Don't call me again here, you understand? I won't take your call if you do. I'll try to give you a ring around---" but the line went dead before he could finish.

What the heck was happening? I hung up the phone and checked the change slot for any extra coins that might have fallen through. *Well, I have nothing planned for tonight, so I'll just wait for his call.*

After work, I sat in the Union with Ben, sipping a cup of hot tea as I told him of the phone calls.

"I just don't understand what is going on. What do you think?" I asked him.

He shook his head and shrugged. "I don't know. But I hope he calls tonight. Say, you wouldn't mind if I brought

25

a pizza by your place later. I'd sure like to be there when he calls."

"That would be great," I nodded. "How about around 6:30? It'll give me a chance to unwind a little first." I gazed out the window at the rain pounding steadily on the streets and sidewalks.

****

"Your pizza, miss," Ben declared in an exaggerated Italian accent. At precisely 6:29, he stood at the front door with an enormous pizza balanced on one hand, like a waiter bringing it to your table.

"We'll never be able to eat all that. Why did you bring such a huge one?"

"Well, I also brought someone to help us eat it."

He stepped quickly into my front room, nodding behind him.

"I hope you don't mind me coming," said a familiar voice. "I tried to tell him we should call and warn you before just dropping in."

"Andy! Come on in. We'll have a mini-party," I exclaimed.

They both crowded onto the mat inside the door and tugged off their soaked shoes. I marveled at Andy's balancing act as he managed to stay on the mat and kick off his shoes while holding two large paper bags. I gathered their dripping jackets and hung them in the bathroom over the tub. Back in the living room, Andy stepped from the kitchen with three open bottles of beer followed by Ben juggling a stack of paper plates and napkins. I motioned

26

towards the cluttered coffee table as I hurriedly stacked up the magazines for the warm pizza box.

The "Smothers Brothers" record album had them laughing more than eating, especially at Ben's imitations of Tommy Smothers. "Mom always liked you best," he quipped, as I wiped tears of laughter from my eyes. Andy shook his head and stuffed in another bite of pizza just as the phone rang. Everyone stopped in mid-laugh as it rang a second time. Ben lifted the tone arm over the record as I headed for the phone. Andy closed the lid on the pizza and sat quietly sipping his beer. I grabbed the receiver.

"Hello?" I said tentatively.

"Lorie, Geoff here. Can you talk?"

Chapter Four

The Stanger

Andy perched on the edge of the couch and Ben sat on the floor by the coffee table watching as I shifted from one foot to the other with my ear pressed to the receiver. I motioned them to come closer. "It's him." They crowded around as I tipped the receiver away from my ear so they could hear. There seemed to be a lot of voices and music in the background. "You're calling from a friend's house?" I asked.

"I can't call from home," Geoffrey Watson said, pausing. "They may be watching."

"What are you talking about? They who?"

"I can't talk about Gustave Whitehead or Weisskopf or whatever his name is because if they think I am, I could lose my job," hissed Watson in a shouted whisper. "Ever since I discovered the Contract, I've been trying to find a way to tell someone who would appreciate the truth."

I glanced at Ben and Andy who both looked back with puzzled expressions.

"What Contract are you talking about?" I asked.

"The Contract between the museum and---hey, wait a minute. Why exactly should I tell you?"

"I'm investigating flights Whitehead made in 1901 before the Wright Brothers' 1903 flight. You are the one who mentioned some Contract," I reminded him.

"Those flights were never verified. Ask anyone and they'll deny they ever happened. You'll have a hard time proving them. What's your interest in all of this anyway?"

I explained about the discovery at Grandmother's house and how I wanted to write a story about it for History's Mysteries to launch my writing career. The line went silent.

I was worried that the connection might have been lost. "Geoff? Geoff? Are you still there?"

He sighed. "If I send you a photocopy of the Contract, can you guarantee that it won't fall into the wrong hands? You're not a professional writer. Besides, you're a woman and you could get hurt. No. It's just too dangerous. I can't."

"Geoff, what do you mean because I'm a 'woman' you won't send it?"

"You know there aren't that many women journalists out there. Nobody's going to believe you talking about a guy beating out the Wright Brothers because, well, it's a question of credibility. You're a girl, probably not a pilot and you don't work around planes. Now I'm not trying to be insulting or anything. That's just the way it is."

"How dare you! Send me a copy of that Contract and I'll show you credibility! Besides, if I use my initials instead of a first name, who will know I'm a woman?"

"I'll have to think about it. If I do send you a copy, it'll be in a plain envelope with no return address. You can't tell anyone where you got it."

"I won't tell a soul. Just send it." I spelled out my address to him. "Now, what exactly is this Contract about?"

In the background, someone slammed a door and loud angry voices seemed to be arguing, followed by Geoff's muffled voice, as if he covered the phone receiver with his hand. With an out-of-breath voice, he spat out, "Listen, I gotta go. Now, don't call me again. Please." Click. The dial tone hummed in my ear.

I held the receiver for several seconds, mostly because my right forefinger was tangled in the black coil of the phone cord. *Wow. What have I gotten myself into?* Then, shaking my head, I hung up the receiver. Everyone drifted back to the living room. The couch and coffee table were strewn with dirty paper plates, wadded napkins, and empty beer bottles. A lone slice of pizza stuck to the bottom of the open box.

Ben collected beer bottles and stacked the empty plates. "Do you think he'll send the Contract?" He piled several empty bottles in his arms and headed for the kitchen.

"I don't know," I replied. "But I wonder what could be so secret that he won't talk about it."

"Sounds like that Contract is between the Smithsonian and someone else," Andy said. "And if he works for the Smithsonian, it would figure it's something they don't want anyone to know about because it might be embarrassing or damaging to the Museum. That would be my guess. Sounds like he might have found out about it by mistake. They must not know he has a copy. If they did, they'd fire him...or worse."

I nodded in agreement as Andy slid the Smothers record back into its jacket. "I think you're right. By the way, is there any way I can get a look at that letter your Uncle Henry wrote?"

"You mean this one?" He grinned as he pulled a folded paper from his pocket and offered it to her.

I took it and held my breath as I unfolded it. The dark copy, printed in block capitals, looked like something

30

a first grader might write. Most of the words were spelled right but the letters were blurred, uneven and smudged. I read it twice, my heart pounding in my ears.

August 3, 1912

Dear Mr. Whitehead,

I hope you won't be mad when you find out about Phil and Bruce hiding No. 22. They done it so it wouldn't get burnt up with the other things those men took from you and were killed for their trouble. I hear people say you lost that trial because you was a German person and people are afraid of you. It's not fair. I know where No. 22 is because I watched the two boys hide it. It is safe and I won't tell no one. I'm really going to miss working at your shop but I have to go away for a while.

Your friend,

Henry Andrew Jackson

I stared at the letter. "Wow. Your Uncle wrote this? I'm surprised he could read at all back then. Can I keep this?"

"I made it for you. Ben said you wanted a copy," he replied. "Yes, he wrote that when he was about 12 years old. He learned to read mostly on his own. Even then, he was a smart guy." He shook his head as if he couldn't believe it either. "I have to tell you, this evening I've had more fun with you two than with anyone since I've been at school this year. Thanks for including me."

I want to hug him, or shake his hand or something, but I just can't. It might embarrass him. Instead, while they put on their coats, I chattered non-stop to be careful driving in the storm and told them I'd let them both know the instant I received the Contract. As I wrote down Andy's telephone number in my address book, we all agreed to keep this whole thing just among the three of us.

At the front door, Andy raced through the rain to his VW but Ben leaned over and kissed me on the cheek before stepping outside into the rain. He is the best friend anyone could have, I thought, as he closed the door. He pushed it back open and leaned inside.

"Hey, if you don't have any plans tomorrow after work, maybe we could grab a cup of coffee at that new deli in town."

"Gee, I'd love to but this has been a long, hard week. I really planned on just staying in and maybe soaking in a nice steamy bath," I said. He started to say something, but I raised my hand. "Alone, Ben. Alone. Maybe another time."

"Yeah. Another time." He shrugged and jammed his hands into his coat pockets before jogging into the rain towards the VW.

I flipped on the front yard light and peeked through the curtain near the doorway at Andy's car pulling away. His red tail lights glowed as he inched through the pouring rain to the corner and turned west. A larger dark car approached from the corner, passed him and slowed at the curb across the street. The headlights blinked off before it had come to a complete stop. *Who could that be at this hour?* I watched and waited but no one got out. Squinting, I tried to identify the figure in the driver's seat through the rain and darkness, but all I could make out was a black mass behind the wheel. The three-story mansion on the far corner was the only other house on the street with a light on besides mine. *If he were going there, he would have parked closer, especially in this weather.*

A shiver crept up my back as I smoothed out the curtain. *I'll just check the doors and windows again to make sure they're locked.* The window in the bathroom was open an inch or two and I snapped it shut, flipping the lock. Satisfied no one could sneak in, I turned off all the lights and crept back to the front room. Through the tiny slit in the curtain, I peeked out at the street at the car looming in the darkness. *It gives me the creeps. What am I afraid of? No one has come up to the door or threatened me. Maybe it's just my imagination.* I tiptoed into my dusky bedroom and closed the blinds.

****

As I put the next-to-the-last book on the finished stack lying beside my typewriter, I yawned. TGIF, finally! I picked up the final volume and started to type the title on the card, The Lost Flights of Gustave... Oh my God! I grabbed the book with both hands. The yellow slip with the name 'Andrew Thomas' printed on it fluttered to the floor.

"It came!" I whispered out loud, staring at the book's cover.

Mrs. Comstock's office door was still closed and the light was on. A young blond girl stepped up to the front desk, smacking her chewing gum as she chomped on it like a cow.

"Hi. Can I help you?" I asked, still clutching the book in one hand as I stepped up to the desk.

"Yeah." The girl leaned over and asked in a low voice, "Where's the john?"

I pointed to the hall just inside the entrance. The girl shrugged and muttered something, then strolled away towards the front door.

I sat back down at my typewriter, still holding the book. I ran my fingers over the embossed words on the cover, "The Lost Flights of Gustave Whitehead" by Stella Randolph. Opening it, my eyes fixed on the 1937 copyright. *This is 30 years old!* I scanned the index and the first few paragraphs, and then thumbed through it, glancing at the pictures: black-and-white photos of a strange, bird-like airplane, with two scalloped wings that folded up. Various people stood or sat in front of it. *That must be his plane called, "Number 22." It looks more like the Leonardo DaVinci drawings of an ornithopter than an airplane. How odd it isn't a bi-plane like the Wright Brothers' Kitty Hawk.* I leafed through the pages looking for a photo of No. 22 in flight, but there was only a newspaper sketch of it flying.

The door to Mrs. Comstock's office clicked shut behind her. I flipped back to the beginning, then turned to the typewriter, removing the card I'd started to type for the borrowed book, hoping the dragon lady would not notice me wasting a card. *This book isn't even supposed to be in this stack.* Books ordered from other libraries went to a different place and were not checked in like the new ones. Out of the corner of my eye, I saw Mrs. Comstock disappear around the corner towards the restroom. I stuffed the Whitehead volume into my oversized purse. *Andy will really be interested in this one. Besides, it came in with his name on it, so if anyone sees me with it, I can say I am delivering it to him.*

At lunch, Ben and I were so busy pouring over the Whitehead book in the Union, we didn't notice Professor Meinz walk up to the table.

"I hope you aren't going to just ignore me?" he said in a most pitiful voice.

"Oh, Herr Meinz," I said, nearly spilling my Coke. "I didn't see you come in!"

"I have that translation for you." He bowed slightly as he handed me the envelope. "A very interesting man, your grandfather."

"That was my great-grandfather Meyer. Wow, I can't believe you got it done so soon." I peered into the envelope. "How could you ever decipher all that tiny script?"

"Once you get used to it, it really isn't that hard. He was a meticulous writer; every letter perfectly formed. Quite the artist. It was really rather fun. Thanks for bringing it to me."

"No. Thank you for taking the time to translate it. I can't wait to read it." I glanced at my watch and stood up. "But I've got to get back to work, so I guess it'll just have to wait until tonight. Thanks a bunch, Herr Meinz."

"Looks like you'll be doing nothing but reading this weekend," commented Ben, eying me as I leafed through the stapled pages.

"Say," I said, "would you do me a big favor and tell Andy about the book coming in and see if maybe you guys could stop by tomorrow so I can give it to him?"

"Sure. I've got to get to the Laundromat tomorrow morning but later I could make it over for lunch. Maybe we could pack some chicken and find a nice secluded park for a picnic."

"Oh, Ben, why 'secluded'," I couldn't resist teasing. "What have you got in mind?"

His face reddened. "I was just thinking about Andy and how he gets so nervous around people. It's probably because he's uncomfortable being seen with us white folks."

"What a thing to say!" I scolded. "Hey, how about we meet at that park down by the river. You know, that one behind the church on Elm Street."

"That would be perfect, as long as the church doesn't have something going on Saturday afternoon. But we could go somewhere else if it's crowded. Shall we say high noon, little lady?" he drawled.

His exaggerated John Wayne imitation made me laugh. "I'll bring the food. You guys bring the Cokes or lemonade. And let's hope it doesn't rain."

Saturday morning, the bright sunlight streaming in through my bedroom window woke me up. I opened the blinds and windows, gulping in the fresh, cool air. Birds chirped and chattered as they flitted about. *What a perfect day for a picnic.*

As I packed the potato salad in individual paper cups, I thought about the journal Great Grandfather William Meyer had written. Last night I'd read the translation explaining how he had left New York soon after his arrival. It seems that he couldn't find work, even with his talent in art and carpentry. He had packed up and moved to Michigan. On the boat coming over from Germany was where he had met Gustave Whitehead, who called himself Gustave Weisskopf. Since William Meyer had known more English, Weisskopf had been eager to practice with him during the long journey.

It disgusted me how the German immigrants had been treated at the turn of the century. Since most of them struggled with English, they lived together in clusters, where they could speak to each other in their native tongue. Meyer had said that most Germans couldn't walk down a single street without being sneered at, spit at, insulted, bullied and cheated. It must have been a depressing way to live.

One entry about how Meyer had helped Weisskopf construct a small model airplane for an exhibit in New York caught my eye. Weisskopf apparently had great ideas but had trouble translating them into the actual plane. That was where great-grandfather had helped, with his artistic

36

eye and knowledge of woodworking. Meyer had been impressed with Weisskopf's knowledge of flight, obtained mostly through his observation of birds and various trial-and-error glider models. Meyer and Weisskopf had stayed together for almost a month after arriving in New York before Meyer left for Michigan, where he married and settled. He had lost touch with Weisskopf and upon finding the article about Gustav's successful flight of 1901, had clipped it, proud of Weisskopf's accomplishment.

I can't wait to tell Ben and Andy about Whitehead. Goose bumps rose on my arms when I thought about my own flesh and blood having known such a man. But why has no one else ever heard anything about Gustave Whitehead? It's obvious that the Smithsonian knows about him, but why all the secrecy?

I hummed the chorus to "I'm a Believer" as I stuffed a small stack of napkins down into one of the two grocery bags stacked on the kitchen table. *Have I packed enough to eat?* An old wool blanket was neatly folded next to the bags along with the Stella Randolph book and manila folder with the journal translation.

****

The church, across the river, was as deserted as the park. *11:45. I am always early.* Sun shone through the trees and glistened off the meandering river. A few white ducks, quacking loudly, waddled up the bank, edging closer as I spread out the blanket and unpacked the bags. Before I knew it, they had reached the first bag and began pecking at the brown paper. "You bold little devils!" I shouted as I shooed them away. They fluttered and squawked back into the river. Andy's VW pulled up next to my Skylark. The boys emerged with a gallon jug of lemonade and a six-pack of Coke, which they lugged to the blanket. They laughed as

I glared at two ducks that had fearlessly returned to within a couple of yards of the picnic area.

While setting out the chicken, potato salad and popping open a bag of corn chips, I told them the best highlights from the journals. I handed Andy the Whitehead book which he took with a grin. Ben smiled as he listened to me chattering on about the journal.

Twenty minutes later, two other cars pulled up beside Andy's and a couple with two young children headed for a picnic table under one of the budding maples. A pair of teenage girls emerged from the other car and strolled down to the river's edge, tossing stones into the water as they talked and giggled.

We'd almost finished lunch when a mysterious black car with tinted windows crept by, then parked down the street about a block from the picnic area. I stared at it, even after it had stopped. *It sure reminds me of the bad guys' cars in Mission: Impossible.*

Ben nodded at the vehicle. "What's with that car?"

"I'm just a little curious about it," I said. But I couldn't stop watching it as I popped the last bite of my sandwich in my mouth.

Ben seemed overly concerned. "OK, what gives with the car?"

I laughed half-heartedly and told him about the strange car that had parked across the street after they'd left two nights ago.

Even though I shrugged it off and said that I was merely curious as to who the driver was, Ben looked over at Andy. "Come on. Let's mosey over and introduce ourselves. You stay here Lorie."

I started to object but sat back down as the two strode toward the black car. *I really don't want them to get that close. This whole thing feels awfully wrong.*

Ben and Andy were within twenty-five yards of the car, when it slowly rolled away. They started to run after it, but it picked up speed and disappeared around a corner.

Chapter Five

Adversity

"Well, did you at least get a look at that license plate?" I asked.

Ben shook his head as Andy answered. "It was one of those federal plates but I'm not sure about the number. I think there were two 8's, but otherwise, I just can't be sure. I was too surprised just seeing those official plates. You don't see a lot of those around here."

"Why would he be checking out us?" Ben asked me.

"I don't know. What do you think? Maybe he's here to investigate that family or those two girls," I said, nodding towards the other people. I hurriedly began collecting the dirty paper plates and cups, jamming them into one of the paper sacks I'd brought.

"Hey, don't be mad at us," said Ben. "Besides, you don't know those other people."

"But why would the government be watching us?" asked Andy.

"Oh, I don't know. Maybe it had something to do with Geoffrey Watson." I spit out the name as if it tasted bitter. "He seemed just a little angry on the phone last night. Remember all that screaming and yelling in the background during the call? It could have had something to do with that. I don't think we had better hang around here, though." *I can't help wonder if that car was the same one that staked out my house last night...*

"Why spoil our picnic? I've got a Frisbee in the car. It's such a beautiful day. Let's stay. Besides, that guy is gone. I don't think he'll come back," said Andy.

Ben stomped on a loose napkin that threatened to flutter away. "You've got a Frisbee? Well, go get it!"

"You boys go on. I want to get this food put away before the ants discover it," I sighed.

After stuffing the bag of picnic remnants in the trunk of my car, I wandered back towards the river's edge. Ducks on the opposite bank, splashed noisily into the river when they saw me. Their quacking and comic walk reminded me of old cartoons. I laughed out loud as they waddled my way. "All right, fellows," I told them. "I saved you a little tidbit." From my pocket I withdrew leftover biscuits and flung the crumbled tidbits towards the approaching flock.

Ben and Andy stopped tossing the Frisbee and jogged over. I giggled at the quacking mass that pushed and shoved for the treats.

"Hey, I almost forgot," said Andy. "What are you guys doing for Spring Break? It's hard to believe Easter falls in March this year."

Ben flipped the Frisbee straight up in the air, and then caught it behind his back as it fell. "I'm headed back to Indiana. My grandparents insist we all spend Easter together."

"I haven't really decided," I told them, upending the bag of crumbs amongst the remaining ducks.

"I had a thought," said Andy. "I'm headed for Fairfield, Connecticut, where my Aunt Darlene lives. That's near Bridgeport. Her dad is Henry Andrew Jackson, my great-uncle, who wrote that letter. There's a chance he might be there for Easter. I was going to invite you both to

41

come on out with me." Then he looked down at the ground. "But I'll understand if you can't."

"Go to Bridgeport?" I blurted. "Your great-uncle might be there? I didn't know he was still alive!"

"Oh yeah, he's still alive but he doesn't live around there, so I've only seen him a couple of times. And he never lets anyone know when he'll come for a visit; he just shows up. You think you might want to come?" Andy asked me.

"Do you think your Aunt would mind?"

"Naw. Aunt Darlene loves kids. She has one of those enormous old houses with about ten bedrooms so you won't have to get a motel or anything. My cousin Burlus is picking me up Friday afternoon and he could probably give you a ride," offered Andy.

What an opportunity to visit Gustave Whitehead's old stomping ground! I walked to the trash can and tossing in the crumpled biscuit bag. *If I could actually interview his Uncle Henry and if he actually saw one of Whitehead's flights, it could be the proof I need to get this story in print. He might even have old pictures.*

Ben pointed to a large dark cloud that had mysteriously appeared overhead. "Hey, I think it's going to rain again. We'd better pack it up before the downpour. I'll get the lemonade jug if you'll bring the blanket, Andy."

Andy and Ben trotted off to clean up the rest of the picnic area while I opened my trunk, making sure I had the book and manila envelope. *I don't really want to go to Andy's in his cousin's car because then I'd have no transportation while I was there. Besides, it'd feel awfully uncomfortable being the only white person in the negro home. But how can I tell him without hurting his feelings? I just can't pass up this opportunity to meet Henry Jackson. He could turn out to be my ace in the hole.* I turned to tell him I would accept his

42

invitation but drive my own car instead. But before I could, Andy cursed, pointing at his lopsided VW, parked just behind me.

"I can't believe it! I just put new tires on this last month. How could two of them be flat already?" he ranted.

Ben knelt down by the left back flat and ran his hand over the tire. Then he went up to the front flat and looked closely at it.

"These tires didn't just go flat. They've been slashed. You must have some pretty powerful enemies," said Ben, shaking his head.

Andy stood staring at the tires and shaking his head.

I offered them both a lift back to my place so Andy could call for a tow truck, but he insisted on being dropped back at the college. During the short hop over to the campus, Andy sat hunched in the back seat, in silence. Raindrops plopped, one at a time, on the windshield as I pulled up to the Student Union. He opened the car door before I had come to a complete stop.

"Andy!" I said, louder than I had intended.

"What?" he barked back.

"I really want to go to your Aunt's for spring break but---"

"Oh, I understand. You don't have to explain. Thanks a lot for lunch," he muttered, leaping out and slamming the door. With his hands jammed in his jacket pockets, he ran through the gentle rain into the Union.

"I thought you wanted to go," Ben said to me.

43

"I do. I was just going to explain about wanting to drive my own car instead of hitching a ride with his cousin. I want to be able to get around once I'm there. Besides, I may not stay the whole week, so if I drive, I can leave early if I want to. But he wouldn't give me a chance to tell him that."

"He's pretty upset about those tires. He probably doesn't have a lot of money for new ones," said Ben. "Hey, let's go grab a cone at Dairy Queen. You never did get to tell me about that Stella Randolph book you got at the library yesterday."

He picked it up off the front seat and began leafing through it.

"Oh rats, Ben. Andy forgot to take the book. Well, that'll give me an excuse to call him later and tell him that I'd love to go there for Easter," I said. "Besides, it will give him a chance to calm down a bit."

But who could have done such a thing to his VW? Those people in the park wouldn't have messed with his car and the black government one with the mysterious driver had left.

I eagerly related parts of the book to Ben at the picnic table outside of Dairy Queen, as we watched the spring rain. As 4:30 drew near, I dropped him at his place and headed for home. For some reason, I was totally exhausted. *Maybe it's all that fresh air. Or maybe it's just the uncertainty about the government car and Andy's split tires.* Whatever the reason, I couldn't wait to soak in a hot bubble bath, and then watch "<u>The Man From U.N.C.L.E.</u>"

I yawned as I flipped the porch light switch. Darkness. The bulb looked OK, from where I stood, flipping it on and off several times. *Guess it's time to change it.* I unlocked the front door. *Everything seems so still. Too still.*

Goosebumps rose on I arms as the door swung open. I stepped inside, shut the door and threw the deadbolt.

When I turned on the kitchen light, I noticed an empty plastic tumbler by the sink. The bread knife lay on the cutting board amidst a mass of crumbs. *I know I left the kitchen spotless. Someone has been here and helped themselves to a sandwich and a drink.* Setting the paper bag on the table, I began opening the cupboard doors. *Things have been moved around but nothing seems to be missing. Oh God, what if he's still here!?*

I tiptoed into the bedroom. The dresser drawers gaped open; underwear and sweaters were pulled part way out or crumpled on the floor. Yanking the closet door open, several blouses hung crookedly on their hangers. Pants and dresses lay in a heap on the floor. I dashed to my jewelry box, relieved that my secret stash of cash was still intact along with my pearls and my Grandma's diamond broach. *Everything of value is still here but someone has definitely been searching for something.* My heart pounded as I peered under the bed and in all the other closets. *Thank Goodness! Nobody is here.*

However, when I stepped into the bathroom, the wet window curtain whipped in through the open window, spraying rain across the floor. I slid across the slick tiles, squinting against the blowing rain, and pulled the window shut, latching it firmly. *What if I'd been here when the burglar had come in?* A shiver ran up my spine as I knelt, drying the cold floor with a wadded-up bath towel. *I should call the police. But nothing has been taken or damaged. Thank goodness for that.* The absurd scene of a burglar with a mask carefully putting things back and closing doors behind him flashed through my mind. *This is crazy! He hadn't wanted to rob me or he would have taken the jewelry and cash. What was he looking for?*

I picked up the phone to dial Ben's number. The line seemed dead with no dial tone, perhaps because of the storm. Then, in my ear, a harsh, whispering voice rose out of the receiver.

"Leave it alone! Watson has no contract. Forget it. Whitehead is nothing to you. Don't pursue it if you value your home and friends. Forget about it."

Then, with a click, the dial tone droned in my ear. I stared at the receiver. *Did I really hear it or not? The caller's slight British accent seemed put-on, like he was trying to disguise his voice. Maybe he thinks I might recognize him.*

I haven't mentioned Watson to anyone other than Andy and Ben. They certainly wouldn't discuss it with anyone else, so how does this stranger know about the conversation with Watson? Had the phone Watson had called from been bugged? Then a horrible thought occurred to me as I stared at the telephone. *Or was my own phone bugged?* I slowly hung up the receiver and stepped back away from it as if it were alive. Staring at it for a minute, I realized I probably wouldn't recognize a phone bug if I were looking right at it. I couldn't take the chance. *Ben won't mind it if I just drop in.*

Snatching my purse, I threw on my rain coat. As I started to unbolted the front door, I suddenly remembered the book and translation and ran back to the kitchen, where they sat, safe in the picnic sack. I tucked them inside my coat and headed for the front door.

****

His house was only a few blocks, but it seemed to take forever to get there. Ben's roommate, Frank, motioned me inside, and then stood in the doorway to the kitchen, his hands wedged in the pockets of his dark blue jeans. *It's funny to see him dressed so neatly in a pull-over Polo shirt*

46

and non-ragged jeans. He actually has combed his shoulder-length hair.

Ben sat on the threadbare maroon-and-tan couch holding a bag of frozen corn to the back of his head. He lowered it only an instant to show me the nasty lump behind his right ear.

"What happened to you?" I blurted.

"Well, after you dropped me off, I stopped at my car in the driveway to pick up a book I'd left on the front seat." Ben winced as he repositioned the bag. "When I closed the car door, someone hit me from behind. Next thing I remember, Frank was kneeling beside me wondering if I was OK. He helped me into the house and gave me the cold pack. I'm OK. I didn't see anyone at all but whoever did it, didn't take my wallet or keys or anything. Even my book was still on the driveway."

Frank stood watching, shaking his head. "I didn't see who hit him either. Ben was lucky that I was even home. I was running late for an appointment and rushing out when I saw Ben lying in the driveway." He looked at his watch and grabbing a jacket off the hook by the door, waved. "Listen, since you're here, I've got to get going before I'm too late."

Ben slid over on the couch, leaving room for me to sit. "So, why are you here, Lorie?"

I sat beside him and told him about the break-in at my house and the strange phone call.

"This is getting too weird, Lorie. Maybe we should call the police." Ben stared down at the bag of corn in his hands. "Assault is a crime. He could have killed me. It's just plain strange that he didn't even take my wallet."

"Yes, maybe we should report it. But I can't find anything missing from my house so I can't even prove there was anyone there in the first place. And as for that phone call, well, who would believe that?"

"I, for one, can't wait for the Spring break to get away from all of this. Do you have Thursday and Friday off next week?" he asked.

"As a matter of fact I do, but now I'm thinking about maybe trying to get Wednesday too. I think since classes are done this week, things should be pretty quiet at the library all next week. I'd sure like to start the trip a day early."

"So you're really going to keep on with this Whitehead thing after that phone threat?"

"You bet. It was just a scare tactic anyway, don't you think?"

"I don't know," Ben answered. "Maybe we should have some sort of code that would alert me if you were in trouble. So if I called when you were in a tight spot, all you'd have to say would be that word or phrase and I'd know something was wrong. I know! You're always teasing me about liking the Cubs by saying, 'How about those Tigers?' That would be perfect."

I laughed but agreed.

****

Monday morning, March 20th, found Ben, Andy and me huddled around steaming cups of hot chocolate in the Student Union just after 7:00 a.m. As we sat in our favorite booth watching a student in an apron swab each table quickly with a damp rag, the rain beat steadily against the dark windows beside us.

48

"So, you're driving up to my Aunt's on Wednesday?" Andy asked me. "Burlus is coming here on Thursday and I've already made plans to go with him, but I can give you directions on how to get there. You're not driving straight through, are you?"

"Of course not. I'll stay over one night," I replied, sipping my warm drink.

"Burlus always travels non-stop because we take turns driving. We'll probably arrive about the same time," said Andy. "I'm so glad you're coming. I sure hope Uncle Henry shows up. He usually does around Easter. Man, you're going to love all my cousins. They're a riot!"

I was glad Andy was excited about me going to his Aunt's. Ben, on the other hand, seemed unusually quiet, staring at his Styrofoam cup.

When there was a momentary pause in the conversation, he turned to me, "Are you sure you want to make that trip alone? I'm not so sure that's such a good idea, what with all that's been happening. Isn't there someone who could go with you? What about Carol, Anita, Diane or Rondi?"

I smiled. "Oh, I'll be all right. They've got their own Spring Break plans anyway. I've taken trips like this before. I can take care of myself. I'm a big girl now, Ben. Besides, I don't think there will be any strange vehicles following anyone, especially if we are all leaving in different cars and at different times."

It's nice to know someone cares. But how does he get off thinking I can't take care of myself? Maybe he's just jealous because he can't go too. That wasn't like Ben, though.

The day progressed at a snail's pace. With most of the students already off on Spring Break, the library was still as a graveyard. Unfortunately new books continued to stack up and needed to be processed, so the place stayed open part of the week. Mrs. Comstock reluctantly granted me Wednesday off with the understanding that I would return by the following Thursday after Easter. Classes didn't resume until two weeks after Easter, April 7th. Most of the rest of the day, I made mental notes about what I needed to pack so that when I went home, I could whiz right through it.

As I scurried around the house that evening, gathering items for the trip, I happened to pause by the front window to lay a magazine on the small end table. I blinked twice, not believing I was really seeing that same sleek black car parked across the street with the lights off. When I went to the window to pull the curtain shut, the vehicle rolled away from the curb and down the street, still with its lights off. *Well, at least it's gone. But why would anyone be watching me? I'll just have to make sure I don't mention this to Ben, or he'll freak.*

****

Tuesday night, with everything neatly packed and sitting by the front door, I sat at the kitchen table with the roadmap and highlighted the route to Bridgeport, Connecticut. The most direct way was on Highway 80 all the way to New York City, then up 84 and 684 to the coast. *I'd rather go along the ocean up to Bridgeport then cut across country. Besides, the address Andy had given me was for Fairfield, which was just south of Bridgeport, on the water, according to the map.* I placed a dark "X" half way across Pennsylvania amidst a small cluster of tiny towns, where I could to stop for the night. *I'll simply have to play it by ear exactly where to stop. Who knows? I might make it as far as Milton.*

Car lights flashed across my living room then disappeared, as if someone had flipped a switch. When I looked around the curtain, the mysterious car was back across the street, with the lights off. *I should march right out there and confront this character.* But before I could open the door, the car pulled away again, vanishing down the dark street. *Good riddance.* I folded the map and yawned. 4:00 came early and I was determined to be on the road by 4:30.

****

My eyes popped open in the blackness. A dog barked in the distance but that couldn't have awakened me. I held my breath and listened. Soft footfalls in the tall grass behind the bedroom window melted away. I rolled silently out of bed and on hands and knees crawled to the window sill, before peering over. *Nothing.* I stood cautiously. A car door slammed, startling me and making me hit my knee on the wooden bed frame. By the time I hobbled to the front room window and pushed the curtain aside, the black car was pulling away from the curb and heading down the street, again with no headlights.

I released the curtain, a sudden chill making me fold my arms tightly across my chest as I shuffled back to the bedroom and climbed back into bed. The clock on the night stand glowed 3:30. *How long has he been wandering around outside?* I sighed and shivered, pulling the covers up over my ears. *Well, at least he's gone. In a short time, I'll be gone too. Then I won't have to give him a second thought.*

Chapter Six

Journey

Much to my delight, the day began bright and sunny. Settled on Highway 80, I cruised along, the radio playing *"Louie, Louie"* higher than my Mom would have allowed. I glanced at my watch: *7:30. My stomach growls, probably because I haven't eaten breakfast yet.* As I passed the first exit for South Bend, Indiana, a Stuckey's billboard, displaying mouthwatering pictures of their chocolate-pecan fudge, declared five more miles before the exit. I licked my lips and decided to pull off there.

My tan '66 Buick Skylark followed a red semi-truck off the exit ramp. *I guess I'm not the only one who's hungry.* I noted in the rearview mirror that several cars trailed behind me into the restaurant lot. An older Chevy with Michigan plates pulled into the space beside me and an elderly couple emerged warbling a cheerful, "Good Morning." I stepped ahead and held Stuckey's front door open for them.

The scent of chocolate fudge, fried potatoes, baked bread and strong coffee hit me as I stepped into the gift shop at the entrance to the restaurant. Shelves were crowded with souvenirs, toys, various candy bars, and gum, among the racks of postcards. Near the cash register counter stood a glass case brimming with trays of chocolate, maple, peanut butter and vanilla nut fudges.

I walked up behind the elderly couple standing by the "Please Wait to Be Seated" sign. A swirl of stale cigarette smoke crept around me, almost making me sick to my stomach. I glanced back at a young, dark-haired, man dressed in tan slacks with a dark brown corduroy sports coat just as he threw his cigarette on the floor and ground it out with the sole of his shiny penny loafer. He blew out one last smoky breath and flashed me a dull smile, then turned away to examine a carved statue of a black bear climbing a tree on a nearby shelf. *What a shame his teeth are so yellow. He could be quite a handsome fellow if he didn't smoke.*

A buxom, uniformed woman clutching a stack of menus approached me. "Table for one or are you waiting for someone?"

"Oh, just one, please."

Since the place was moderately crowded, the hostess led me to a small booth near the back, looking out into the parking lot. I perused the breakfast page of the menu, humming along with an instrumental version of "I Can't Get No Satisfaction" playing faintly over the loud-speaker.

A moment later, a large, gray-haired waitress stopped at my table and flipped the coffee cup upright in the saucer. "Coffee, Honey?"

I nodded and ordered the No. 1 Special. The woman poured the cup full almost to the brim, then plopped the pot on the table before scribbling on her pad. After stuffing the tablet into her apron pocket while sliding the pencil behind her ear, she snatched up the pot and stepped to the table behind me.

A familiar odor of stale smoke drifted into my booth. I wrinkled my nose, and wondered if it was the same young man. But I didn't want to turn around and have to talk to him, so I simply straightened my back and stared out at the parking lot, listening to his voice as he ordered. I could feel his eyes on me. When the waitress finished writing and scurried back past my table, I put out my hand to stop her.

"Excuse me, where is the lady's room?"

"Right behind you, honey," said the waitress, indicating with the jerk of her thumb the "Restrooms" sign at the rear of the room.

"Thanks," I muttered. I stood and slung my purse over my shoulder.

Glancing nonchalantly as I hurried past the man's table, I noticed him nod and smile. *He seems pleasant enough, but there is something unsettling about his eyes.*

I washed my hands in the restroom, thinking how much I hated sitting with my back to him. *Well, I certainly won't take the opposite seat or I might have to talk to him.* Pulling down the cloth towel to a fresh spot, I blotted my hands. *Just eat quickly and get back on the road again.* I rapidly walked by him and slid back into the booth. He seemed too engrossed in his newspaper to notice me this time.

Only moments later, the waitress appeared with a steaming plate of bacon and eggs, fried potatoes and a small plate of toast. Before I could refuse, my cup was filled once again to the brim. She wedged my bill under the saucer of individual jam and jelly packets, before stepping back with his order.

I had been hungrier than I'd thought, digging into the heap of potatoes. *I'll never be able to eat it all.* I was surprised as I pushed the last bite of egg onto my fork with a toast corner. With a rustle of paper, the man behind clattered his coffee cup in his saucer and I heard him slide out from the booth. *Man, he must have really been hungry to have finished before me!* He walked by, not glancing my way. I looked out into the lot, curious as to which car was his, but he never appeared. *He must have parked over on the other side.* I shrugged off an uneasy feeling I had about this mystery man, put a few coins on the table for the waitress and took my bill to the front.

Outside, the sun hid behind a gray cloud, looking like it might rain at any moment. I pulled back onto the highway, watching for directions towards Toledo. The traffic had picked up since I'd pulled off, so I had to concentrate on driving more than before. In my rear view mirror, a black Fury cruised behind for several miles, but hung back far enough, I couldn't make out the driver. Then, when I looked back a few moments later, the car was gone, although I could have sworn it didn't pass me. *It must have pulled off.*

Deciding not to stop for lunch at a restaurant, I had packed a few sandwiches, chips, two apples and four bottles of Coke. Akron, Ohio loomed in the distance, but I had no desire to head into any cities and risk getting lost. I vowed to stay on 80 or close to it for the whole trip. There were plenty of roadside rest stops---the next one was in two miles. *Perfect. I can't wait to stretch my legs.*

The sun peeked out from behind a dark cloud and shone brightly as I exited. Although most people parked close to the concrete block restroom, I chose a space further away near a cluster of picnic tables. As I unpacked lunch on a table beneath a large tree, squirrels scampered on the overhead limbs and around the trunk. I ate, trying to concentrate on the paperback I'd brought, but was too distracted by small children chasing a Frisbee and dog-walkers being pulled by their canines. Chirping birds and the sun creeping through the leaves made me sigh and I put my head down on my arms, deciding to rest my eyes for a few minutes. I jerked awake, eyeing my watch. *I've been asleep for almost 15 minutes!* I grabbed my purse and stretched my arms over my head. Then I took off at a swift pace across the yard towards the restrooms.

As I rounded the corner of the building to the "Women" side, I saw the suited, dark-haired man from the restaurant again flip another cigarette onto the sidewalk and grinding it out. *What in the world is he doing here? It seems unbelievable that it could just be a coincidence.* I watched as he headed towards the lot. Then, he abruptly stopped, turned and smiled right at me. I inhaled sharply and stepped back into the restroom. *It definitely wasn't a coincidence! This guy has been following me.* I slowed my breathing until my heart beat normally. But when I finally poked my head back out, hoping to catch a glimpse of his car, he had disappeared. *The only car leaving its space is a black Fury, a lot like the one that had parked outside my house earlier. I can't quite make out the license plate or who the driver is.* I turned back into the restroom and splashed cold water on my face.

Back on the road, I checked the rear-view mirror twice as often and watched drivers as they passed. No black car like the Fury showed up. As the highway driving settled into a smooth ride, I yawned again. Singing loudly with the car radio and chewing gum until my jaw ached helped me stay awake.

Passing over the state line into Pennsylvania, I passed Greve City, Clarion, Du Bois and Clearfield before pulling into a filling station near the turnoff to Bald Eagle State Park. While the attendant filled the tank and checked the oil, I headed for the main building. Rows of snacks, candy and a cooler of beer and pop were crammed into the tiny space. After checking the isles twice, I chose a bag of cheese puffs and a frosty bottle of Verners ginger ale, popping its top off with the opener on the wall by the register before heading back to the car. Three vehicles had pulled up to the pumps while I'd been inside. A tall, thin man in a business suit stood beside a white Cadillac watching the attendant wash his front windshield. Both driver's seats in a red Mustang and a rusty, blue Ford pickup at the other pumps were empty. The attendant and the businessman stopped talking and stared at me as I eyeballed the two cars. When I noticed them watching me, I shrugged and smiled, then slid back into the car, and started the engine.

Traffic slowed down around Williamsport by 5:30, so best not stop there, in spite of my growling stomach. Motel signs for the Muncy exit looked inviting, reminding me how tired I really was, so I exited, winding back over the freeway towards a cluster of buildings. With no one behind me, I cruised down the main street, pulling in the AAA-approved Blue Moon Motel. After checking in and setting my suit-case in the clean, modest room, I put on my windbreaker and headed down the sidewalk towards the Blue-Lite Diner in the second block.

The streetlights glowed brighter as the sun sank lower on the horizon with each step. Everything had closed except the Blue-Lite, a brightly lit Laundromat across the street, and neon flashing beer bottle on a bar further down. Faint country music and bursts of laughter emanated from the bar, but a quiet dinner and an evening in front of the TV interested me more. A bell jingled as I entered the restaurant, the smell of fried food and cigarette smoke heavy in the air.

The place wasn't exactly packed. Two farmers in overalls and plaid shirts with their heavyset wives, along with a couple of elderly men huddled in the back booths. Three young, jean-clad men perched at the counter, one buried in his newspaper and two jabbering to each another. When I walked in, they abruptly fell silent. I could feel them stare as I made my way to an empty table by the window.

Zipping my jacket up all the way, I tried to dispel the sensation of being watched. When I glanced at the men at the counter, they lowered their voices, but continued to eye me, from time to time bursting into laughter.

The speaker right above my head crackled out a twangy-voiced singer and a frantic fiddler. *Certainly not my first choice in music.* Less than five minutes from when I'd ordered the Blue Plate Special, it arrived. A heavy plate of Salisbury steak, green beans and mashed potatoes swim-ming in glistening gravy was plopped in front of me, followed by a sparse bowl of brown-edged lettuce with a single cherry tomato beside three rubbery carrot sticks, smothered in French dressing. Somehow, I just wasn't as hungry as I'd originally thought. Only three bites later, I set my fork down, wiped the edge of my mouth with a paper-thin napkin and grabbed my purse.

When I stepped back outside onto the sidewalk, I gulped in the cool breeze that whipped though my hair. My sandals clacked as I hurried back towards the motel. Pausing at the corner at the end of the first block, I thought I heard footsteps behind and glanced over my shoulder. The street was empty. I trotted across to the other side, my breathing and pounding heart thumping in my ears.

The blue crescent moon on the motel sign ahead seemed reassuring. A dark car crept down the street and I paused to watch it at an intersection. Again, the echo of footsteps made me turn and stare into the shadows. A shadowy figure disappeared around the corner in the previous block and all was silent. My purse clutched at my side, I jogged the final block to the parking lot of the motel, fumbling to unzip my purse as I rummaged for the key before remembering I'd stuffed in it my jacket pocket. My hand shook as I jammed the key in the lock and snapped open the deadbolt. In one motion the door whipped open, I leapt in, banged the door shut and threw the bolt. *Glad I'd thought to leave a light on!* I collapsed onto the bed and lay panting. The heater creaked and groaned as its tepid air blew on my cold face. Too tired for even a relaxing bath, I changed out of my clothes and, climbing into the lumpy bed, pulled the blankets up around my chin.

****

Early Thursday morning, with the map spread out across the steering wheel, I took a sip from a steaming paper cup of coffee and stuffed a stale corn puff into my mouth. *I want to make Stroudsburg, just before the New Jersey state line, before noon. Then I'll have the afternoon to cross New Jersey and maneuver my way through New York City to the coast, hopefully before the rush hour traffic. I'll pick up Highway 1 at New Rochelle and go north along the coast to Bridgeport.* Wiping my corn-puff-orange fingers on a tissue, I folded the map and started the Buick.

The car clock glowed 6:35 as I pulled back onto Highway 80 heading east. The radio weatherman predicted mostly sunny skies with a few intermittent showers in the afternoon. *Great. Rain to deal with while trying to get through New York City.* I turned up the volume and sang along with the Monkees' "I'm a Believer."

Signs for the twin covered bridges at Berwick popped up only an hour and a half later. Since it was only a few miles off the road, I decided to stop there and eat the bag of sweet rolls I'd picked up near the motel. The sun sparkled on the dewy pastures as I bumped along the deserted gravel road. I rounded a bend in the road and the first quaint bridge came into view, perched over a rapidly flowing fork of Susquehanna River. *Far out!* Pulling off the road into a small gravel lot, I gazed at the postcard-perfect bridge.

With my paper bag of rolls, I strolled out onto the white-washed bridge, staying close to the right side railing. My foot falls echoed off the wood planking as I headed towards a built-in bench near the center, peering through small window slots every few yards. Settling on the bench, I unpacked the sweet rolls. In the distance came the unmistakable clip-clop of a horse, growing louder by the minute. I grinned at a towering, dapple gray Belgium, pulling a bale-laden wagon that filled the entire far opening of the bridge. The sweet scent of freshly cut hay filled the tiny enclosure. As the horse plodded by, the elderly farmer holding the reins nodded down at me. I waved back. *Sure would be nice to sit here all morning, beside the slow moving river, just watching the world go by.*

The roar of car engines at the bridge entrance was oddly out of place, snapping me out of my daydream and reminding me that I had a schedule to keep. So I stuffed the last bite of the second sweet roll into my mouth, licked the sticky frosting from my fingers and slugged down the last sip of coffee. Then I crammed the papers and empty cup into the bag. *I'll just rinse off my hands in the cool river before I get back into the car.*

A station wagon loaded with waving and yelling kids thundered over the wood planking as I headed back to the bridge entrance. I nodded at them and strolled along the uneven floor, stopping at a window opening to watch a fish leap out of the river. But, as I turned back towards the entrance, another dark car emerged at the far end of the bridge with its headlights gleaming, coming straight at me. I stayed close to the right on the raised walkway as the car approached. The bridge was plenty wide for it to easily pass, but it seemed to be hugging my side. I held my breath as it roared past, the wind from the close encounter tearing at my jacket. I turned, glaring at the back end of the black car before it disappeared through the exit and up the road. *Crazy driver.*

However, I quickened my pace through the bridge. A flicker of headlights flashed off the inside of the bridge. The car had turned around and roared back towards me. I bounded through the entrance and off the side of the road, stumbling down to the river's edge. All I saw out of the corner of my eye was a glimpse of the black car as it whizzed on up the gravel road, disappearing in a cloud of dust. I sat on a rock jutting out into the river for a few moments, trying to catch my breath. Swishing my sticky hands in the cool water, I also splashed some on my face. *That was way too close!* The icy water stung my nose and eyes, almost taking my breath away. On shaky legs, I climbed up the steep bank to the car. *Had it just been some wild teenagers or had someone actually tried to run me down?* I fastened my seatbelt, certain the car was the same black Fury that I'd seen on the road and at the rest stop. *But who was it and why would he be following me?* I shivered and flicked on the heater as I headed back to Highway 80.

Chapter Seven

Auntie's

I turned at the post marked "28028" and headed up the driveway towards the farmhouse. *This house is huge!* At the top, surrounded by flowering maples, the two-story white farmhouse sat with its wraparound, screened-in porch. A weather-beaten, metal roofed barn stood a short distance away, with whitewashed fencing stretching far down the hill and across what appeared to be the edges of the property. Fields of tall green grasses seemed to go on forever, leaning from the howling wind that swept up from the ocean. The bouquet of wild flowers mingled with salt water air blanketed the hillsides.

I pulled into the farmyard next to a blue, mud caked pickup. Beside it sat a sleek, white Mustang with a sloping fastback. At least someone's here, I thought, climbing out of the car. A flock of chickens skittered across the yard towards me. I stood still as they fluttered past, intent on pecking the bugs and grasshoppers clinging to my car's front bumper and grill.

A screen door slammed and a tall, thin coal-black woman, in a mid-calf navy blue dress sprinkled with white flowers walked out and down the front porch steps towards me. She wiped her hands on her pale blue apron as she approached, then held out her right hand.

"Well, child, you must be Lorie." Her long, slender fingers enveloped my hand with a strong grip. She then followed me around to the trunk. "Andy told me you might beat him and Burlus here. I'm Darlene Peters, but you can call me Auntie. Every-one does. Even to those who aren't family, I'm just plain Auntie. Here," she grabbed up my suitcase, "I'll help you carry your things."

61

"Nice to meet you, Mrs. Peters, I mean Auntie." I pointed at the suitcase. "Oh, I'd better take that—it's pretty heavy."

She set it down with a smile. "Perhaps it is too much for my old back."

"I hope I'm not intruding on your Easter plans," I said. "I was hoping to meet your father."

"Heavens no, child. The more the merrier," said Auntie with a chuckle. "Why, Daddy should be here any time now. You know, he always shows up around Easter. I don't know why. He only occasionally comes on Christmas or Thanksgiving or other holidays, but always on Easter. Here, let me give you a hand with some of your lighter things." She draped a bag of hanging clothes over her one arm and picked up the smaller train case with the other hand. "He always was a mysterious man, my daddy."

I smiled and grabbed the big suitcase along with a paper sack full of shoes. *I really like this lady. She reminds me of my own Aunt Jean.* As we reached the front porch, a large silver Cadillac crackled up the driveway, pulling in beside my Skylark. We turned, watching Andy and another much larger man emerge from the car.

"Lord be praised!" exclaimed Auntie. Plopping my train case down and throwing the clothes over it, she ran down the steps and threw her arms around both of the boys at once.

"Auntie!" they shouted in unison sporting big grins.

"Burlus! Andy! Why---I can't believe how you've grown. Last time you were here, you were just strutting teenagers and now look at you. You've all grown up into fine, handsome men." She held them at arms' length. "Let me look at you."

Andy peered over her shoulder, spotting me standing on the porch. "Hey, you made it! I thought for sure we'd beat you."

He slung his old, green backpack over one shoulder and strode across the yard, taking the porch steps two at a time. I reached out to shake hands and he grabbed my hand, and then let it go quickly. I could feel my face burn and cleared my throat. "I made real good time and the traffic was pretty light."

Andy looked over at Auntie and Burlus chattering by the car and licked his lips. Then he turned and opened the screen door with one hand while grabbing up my suitcase with the other, motioning me to go ahead of him into the house. "We might as well go on in."

When we stepped into the front room, a large, black, balding man walked up to Andy and slapping him on the back, exclaimed in a booming voice, "Andrew Thomas! What a sight for sore eyes! You've grown up into a young man. Say, who's that with you?"

"Uncle Luther, I'd like you to meet Lorie," Andy said, while Uncle Luther and I shook hands. "She works in the library at the college and is here to meet Great-Uncle Henry. Is he here yet?"

"No, but I 'spect he'll show by dinner time Saturday. He usually spends at least a couple of days here at Easter." Luther put his arm around Andy and walked with him towards the dining room table. "Tell me, boy, how is school going?" A young light-colored negro girl was busy setting out the silverware for a meal. Luther paused to tell her, "Lizzie, you be sure to set enough places, you hear?"

I jumped at Auntie's voice from behind. "Where are my manners? Burlus, you grab that suitcase and take it up to James' old room. You know, the one at the far end of the

63

hall on the right? I'm sure she'll want to settle in before supper."

Burlus, a much larger, heavier version of Andy, muttered a respectful, "Yes, Auntie," as he grabbed up my suitcase and led the way up the stairs.

The charming old house fascinated me with its carved moldings and graceful rounded edges. High ceilings gave the hallways and rooms a more spacious feeling than most of the houses today and reminded me of Grandma's Michigan house. I absolutely loved the egg-shaped doorknobs and lacy-patterned, metal vent covers on the walls. Although the carpets were thin and thread-bare in places, they were clean and lacked that musty odor that old rugs usually acquired. We passed several bedrooms and a large bathroom as we made our way down the long hall to the last two rooms.

"Uncle Henry usually stays there, in that room just across from James'," said Burlus, pointing over his shoulder with his thumb. The door to the other room was shut, unlike the other open ones we'd passed.

I thanked Burlus for carrying my suitcase and shut the door after he had left. The double bed with its colorful patchwork quilt, a small mahogany chest of drawers with several wall hooks above it, and a polished writing desk with a high-back chair pushed neatly under it, nearly filled up the small room. From the open window, I looked down on the barn and driveway I'd driven up on, winding even further down and around the rolling hills. I pushed the window up another inch or so, breathing in the pungent salt air. A huge yawn made my ears crack loudly. *What a relief!* I kicked off my shoes off and flopped onto the bed. *With supper only an hour away, I don't feel like unpacking yet, so maybe I'll just rest my eyes for a few minutes.*

****

"LORIE! Are you in there?" came a deep voice accompanied by a loud pounding on the door.

I rolled off the bed, stumbling to catch my balance. Quickly smoothing my blouse, I ran my fingers through my hair and opened the door.

Andy's smiling face greeted me. "It's time for supper. I've been calling you but you didn't answer. Are you OK?

"Yes, yes. I just closed my eyes for a minute. I must have dozed off. I'll be right down."

Andy laughed and shook his head as he ambled back down the hall.

I pulled my auburn hair straight back off my face, securing it with a silver clip on the top, then brushed out the sides and back. I added only a dab of blush and refreshed my lipstick before sliding into my flats. Then, pulling the door closed behind me, I hurried down the hall towards the stairs, afraid I might be late.

Conversation seemed to come to a halt when I arrived. Everyone smiled as I slid my chair out and sat down. After a moment of awkward silence, Uncle Luther introduced me, then cleared his throat and asked Lizzy if she would say grace. The thin girl nodded and bowing her head took the hand of the person on each side. Like dominoes collapsing, everyone followed her lead and joined hands. I tentatively grabbed the young boy's open palm to my right and Andy's hand on the left. A drop of sweat trickled down my back, in spite of the cool, breezy weather. With grace over, dishes were passed and table talk turned to how wet the weather had been and what Burlus and Andy did at school. Nine people crowded around the rectangular table including two young girls I had not seen before. An empty tenth place was set at the far end.

Silverware clattered against plates. Lip smacking and chewing were soon all that could be heard as everyone concentrated on the fried chicken, mashed potatoes, gravy and baby peas. Each time I glanced up, it seemed someone was watching me and I quickly gazed back down at my plate. The longer I sat, the more uncomfortable the chair felt. Beads of perspiration popped out on my forehead and I began to wonder if my hair stuck up somewhere or what, exactly, was wrong with me. Part way through the meal, I wiped my mouth with my napkin and excusing myself, bolted for the second floor bathroom.

In the mirror above the sink, my pale face, washed-out blue eyes and tight lips stared back. *This trip was a big mistake. I really don't belong here. I knew Andy's family and Uncle Henry would all be colored. It's no good. Was this the way Andy felt at school among a sea of white students? How could he have stood to be there as long as he had? Thank goodness I brought my own car. I should just run down and jump in it right now. I haven't unpacked and I could drive into town to a motel.* I gritted my teeth and frowned. *No, that would be rude. I can't do that to Andy. I came here to talk to Uncle Henry and that is what I am going to do!*

I glared in the mirror, lifted my chin and dabbed cold water on my eyes. Then, taking a deep breath and counting each step on the way down the stairs, I straightened my back and walked into the dining room. The low voices and whispers quit as I sat tall in my chair. My heart pounded in the silence.

Andy cleared his throat. "Lorie, I was trying to tell everyone why you're here. Maybe if you explain your interest in Uncle Henry, they'll understand better."

No one moved, almost as if they had all forgotten how to breathe. My voice quivered slightly as I began. But as the story of the discovery in Grandmother's library unfolded, the quaking subsided. Words tumbled out as I described Great-Grandfather's tablet. All eyes were all focused on me

66

and some of them smiled and nodded as I spoke. Uncle Luther interrupted to ask a question about the journal and soon comments erupted like, "That's unbelievable!" and "That's amazing!" I laughed as their questions bombarded me, answering them as fast as I could.

"Here, Lorie, have another piece of chicken," said the teenager sitting beside me, offering the platter. "By the way, I'm Leroy, Andy's cousin."

He grinned as I took the platter from him. "Thanks Leroy, I think I will."

A screen door slammed off the kitchen. Auntie rose from her chair, craning her neck to see who had come in.

"Why, bless my stars! Daddy!" She tossed her napkin on her chair and headed towards the tall, thin man standing in the doorway.

As he grabbed the cap off his snow white head, Auntie threw her arms around his slender body. He lightly hugged her back and smiled. With her arm around him, she walked him to the empty table setting and pulled out his chair. "We saved some of your favorite fried chicken, Daddy. It's so good to see you again," she said. "Oh, where are my manners? This young lady is Lorie Drucker, a friend of Andy's from school. She came all the way here just to see you."

"Nice to meet you, sir," I said, sitting tall in my chair.

Uncle Henry stared at me for a moment before nodding his head with a quick jerk. Then he carefully tucked his napkin in the neck of his red-and-black checkered shirt and under each red suspender before looking down to his plate. He heaped it full, and then ate, calm and quiet, not once glancing up. His family made a few comments to him, but realizing he was not going to respond, soon turned their conversation elsewhere. People began drifting away from the table, while he sat and ate, so when Andy rose to leave the table, I excused myself as well, carrying my plate to the kitchen behind him.

In the living room, the family had gathered around the large TV console. Andy and I watched as an excited newscaster's voice blared from the small screen about students converging on the city of Fort Lauderdale, Florida for their spring break. Flashes of teenagers waving beer bottles and smashing car windows filled the screen as the voice said an estimated 30,000 students were expected to be there. Luther and Auntie both shook their heads and clucked their tongues while the younger people watched with rapt attention.

"Come on, let's get out of here. I'll show you around the farm," whispered Andy.

The back door opened onto a grassy lawn where a clothesline was strung and a picnic table sat beneath a large, thick-limbed oak. The barn loomed off to the side, throwing a dark shadow across the house.

I followed Andy around the side of the house where the garden lay. There were eight to ten rows of freshly tilled ground with wooden stakes at the edge of each furrow labeling what was planted beneath. A chicken-wire fence surrounded it with a flimsy metal gate on one side.

Andy leaned against the trunk of an apple tree at the corner of the garden and stared at the barn. "I remember one Christmas when I was about nine, we had a heck of a blizzard and I sneaked out to the barn through the snow to see a new litter of kittens and bring the mama cat scraps from dinner. I only had on my pajamas and had just stepped into my snow boots. It had been so cold I nearly froze just getting from the house to the barn. The snow came up way higher than my boots and I got half way there and thought about turning back. But I thought about how those kittens were so tiny and the mama cat hadn't had any dinner. So, I plowed through the drifts with all my might. I probably looked like a snowman by the time I came through that barn door." He paused and pulled up a long strand of grass to chew on. "I was so cold by the time I got inside, I forgot to be scared. But I spent all Christmas Eve there, huddled beneath a horse blanket up against Bettes, our cow. The barn had creaked and groaned so in the windy storm, I just knew it was filled with ghosts and I hid under that wool blanket until Uncle Luther found me the next day. I'm still not convinced that big old barn isn't haunted. You sure won't catch me spending any more nights out there."

The sun had almost disappeared as we walked back around to the driveway beside the old gray barn. A tapping sounded from behind its twin sliding doors, one of which stood partly open. Andy motioned me to follow him as he crept towards it, pulling it wider with a loud creak. The tapping stopped as we peered into the dim interior.

A bent over figure hovered over a heavy wooden plank that rested on two bales of hay beside one of the main beams, with his hammer raised as we approached.

"Uncle Henry. What are you doing?" asked Andy.

His Uncle's voice was surprisingly deep and strong as he replied, "Fixin' it."

He pointed down at a faded, wooden figure on the plank before him. I cocked my head one way and then the other, trying to decide what it was. Uncle Henry laid down his hammer and picked up the figure, turning it around until the head with its open beak, that appeared to be screaming, was on top. He looked at Andy and me and simply said, "Rooster."

Andy looked at me and shrugged his shoulders. His Uncle grabbed his arm with one hand and pointed up at the dark ceiling above with the other.

"Weathervane."

Chapter Eight

Henry

Uncle Henry sat on an old metal stool behind his plank workbench, and turned over the faded wooden rooster gently in his hands, smoothing its rough edges with sandpaper. Splotches of red and burnt orange shone through the coarse exterior of the tired bird, which had probably been a grand weathervane in its day.

The old man's bony fingers caressed the wooden statue before laying it down. He motioned for Andy to hand him the paper bag sitting on the end of the plank. Uncle Henry pulled out several small containers of paint and a cluster of thin paintbrushes, arranging them all neatly on the bench.

"I saw an amazing wooden albatross weather-vane for sale down in town just before we got here that would look super on the barn," said Andy.

Uncle Henry met Andy's gaze for a moment before looking away and selecting a small thin brush from the collection. "No."

While the old man pried off the lid of a tiny can of red paint, I reiterated why I had come to visit Andy's family, ending the short narrative with, "Did you really work with Gustave Whitehead? Why did you quit working for him?"

He began painting the rooster with short, measured strokes, spreading the red paint with a steady hand. I (thinking maybe he was a little deaf since he had ignored me) repeated the questions a little louder and slower. Andy interrupted, lightly touching my arm and motioning me to follow him towards the animal stalls on the far side of the barn.

I turned towards Uncle Henry and gave a tiny wave. "Goodbye."

He continued his painting as if we weren't there.

"Why won't he answer me? Is there something wrong with him? Or is it me?" I asked, exasperated.

"Uncle Henry doesn't talk much. Never has. I've only heard him respond with two or three words whenever anyone asks him anything. Listen, you're not family and he probably just feels uneasy, so I'll ask him if he'll talk to you and explain again why you want to know. I don't think now is a good time though. Best to let him be for now. Let's get out of here. I know a good place in town for dessert."

I'm up for that! We walked passed the old man, still dabbing at the bird, towards the barn door. When I glanced back, our eyes met and a chill ran up my spine.

****

At 9:15 in downtown Fairfield that Friday night, Andy and I sat in a booth at the Starlight Cafe, overlooking the ocean. On our table, the lighted candle jammed into a wax-covered wine bottle, flickered each time the door opened and closed. A stout waitress with frizzy gray hair moved from table to table, coffee pot in hand, smiling at the few remaining patrons. The Mills Brothers' "Cab Driver" drifted from the speakers hanging in the corners. Andy tapped his fingers on the table in time to the music. I sat across from him and when the waitress picked up the coffee pot to make her rounds again, I flipped my cup over in its saucer. She made her rounds to every table but ours. *Maybe she didn't see us come in.* The woman walked directly towards us, then passed by and grabbed the ketchup bottle off the table behind.

Andy raised his hand to get her attention but she abruptly turned away and disappeared into the kitchen area. Two other couples left, leaving only a pair of teenage girls giggling together at the counter. An old hunchbacked man wearing a floppy hat littered with fishing flies, the brim pulled low over his eyes, sat at the table closest to the door. Over the top of his newspaper, he leered at the females, although they didn't seem to notice. Then, as the girls grabbed their shoulder bags and headed for the door, the waitress reappeared, heading towards the old man. She lifted the edge of his fishing hat and whispered something in his ear and he responded with a sharp cackle, looking around her at Andy and me, then back at his paper.

The waitress finally strolled over and looked directly at me. "You will have to leave. We're closing up."

She started to walk away when Andy spoke up. "Hey, it's not even nine-thirty. The sign says you're open until ten. What's the deal?"

The waitress spun around and hissed through her teeth, "Sorry, but we're closing early and you have to leave now. Do you understand or should I call the police?"

"The police? All we want is some pie and coffee."

The waitress locked eyes with Andy as she yelled towards the kitchen, "Hey George! We got some trouble-makers out here. You'll have to call the cops."

I scraped my chair back and rose. "Come on, Andy, let's get out of here. This place is no good anyway."

Andy's eyes glistened as he jerked back towards me and stood. He towered over the waitress by at least half a foot. As we filed past the man with the fishing hat, he stared at us with a tight smile and said under his breath, "Trash." Andy slammed the outside door and cursed.

73

With his hands thrust deep in his pants' pockets, he silently walked beside me down the deserted main street in the cool evening air. A few cars were parked beside a brick, three-story hotel on the corner that sported a neon beer sign in the window. Street-lights shone hazily through the fog creeping in from the ocean. I could just barely make out my vehicle parked in the next block. Headlights from behind lit up the sidewalk ahead. But instead of passing, the car slowed and coasted along beside us.

"Oh, my gosh!" I gasped, staring at the sleek black car I'd seen at the covered bridge that morning. *And the driver is the man with the cigarette who was at the restaurant yesterday.* I walked faster, breaking into a jog.

Andy trotted along beside me looking first at the car and then at me. "What's wrong Lorie? You know that guy?"

"He's been following me. He tried to run me down earlier today when I stopped for breakfast."

"You've got to be kidding. Why?"

"I don't know."

When we reached the intersection, Andy grabbed my arm, bringing us both to a halt. We looked over at the grinning driver of the Fury who pointed at me with his finger, like he was shooting a gun, and then laughed, screeching down the street and skidding around the corner.

I crossed my arms and shivered even though I was wearing a warm jacket. "Come on, let's get on back to Auntie's."

Andy opened the passenger door for me, then ran around to the driver's side and unlocked the door. I paused before getting in, snatching a scrap of paper jammed under the front wiper blade. Unfolding it, I read the scrawled words, "Forget Whitehead, Nigger Lover."

74

"What's it say?" asked Andy, turning the ignition key.

"Nothing. Just some old ad," I replied, crumpling it into a tight ball.

I stared out the passenger side window all the way back to his Aunt's house, trying not to blink for fear of tears escaping from my eyes. By the time we pulled into the driveway, my hand ached from squeezing the wadded-up paper.

****

I awoke Friday morning with a start. When I saw the time on my travel alarm, my eyes popped wide open. *10:15! I never sleep in that late.* The aroma of frying bacon drifted up from the kitchen below, making my stomach growl. I jumped out of the bed, stretched and then shuffled down the hall to the bathroom, the cold wood floor creaking beneath my bare feet.

Today could be the day. There has to be a way to convince Uncle Henry to talk about Whitehead. Maybe if I show him the Stella Randolph's book, "Lost Flights of Gustave Whitehead" along with the translation of my Great-Grandfather Myer's journal, he will believe how serious I am about my search for information. I slipped into my red plaid skirt and off-white blouse. *Why won't he talk about it? Is he ashamed of something or is it because I'm white?*

Auntie's bright smile greeted me along with a perky "Good Morning!" as she stood by the stove with spatula in hand. After devouring a pair of over-easy eggs, bacon and hash browns washed down with two cups of coffee, I tucked the Whitehead book under my arm and set out for the barn. I tiptoed through the maze of pecking chickens in the yard, careful not to excite them. *The sky is a brilliant blue this morning, and the mere whisper of a wind seems like an omen*

75

of good things to come. I hummed, pulling open the barn door.

The smell of hay mingled with a faint scent of fresh paint as I stood squinting until my eyes became accustomed to the dim light. A cow mooed softly in one of the back stalls. *I wonder how many animals are housed in this barn. I haven't seen any horses or cows yet.* There, on the workbench, propped up against a box, sat the open-mouthed wooden rooster, his jaunty bright wings and tail feathers life-like. *Uncle Henry has sure done a marvelous job.* I reached out to touch the shiny black beak when I heard a rustle in the straw from behind. Jerking back my hand, I turned.

"Uncle Henry, you startled me. This bird is beautiful. Is he dry yet?"

With a bucket in one hand and a pitchfork in the other, he approached. His faded, patched blue-jeans and thin, white cotton shirt tucked neatly into them, cinched tightly with a narrow leather belt, made him appear almost dressed up. A red bandana handkerchief peeked out from his hip pocket and his worn work boots were polished to a dull shine.

He set the pail down and propped the pitchfork against a beam. "Dry enough to put back up."

He started to drag a long ladder away from the barn wall, so I laid the book on the workbench, ran over, and grabbed the other end. Together we carried it outside and propped it against the longest, tallest side. In amazement, I watched Uncle Henry scoot up the ladder; the rooster tucked under one arm. With the agility of a teenager, he hopped onto the roof and sidestepped up the slope towards the peak. It took him only a moment to affix the rooster weathervane back on its original metal stand. Before he descended, he paused to scan the countryside.

Auntie screamed from the kitchen doorway, "Daddy! Whatever are you doing up there on that barn roof?" He looked down at her and waved towards the weathervane, brightly glistening in the sun. "My stars! He's gone and fixed up that scary, old wooden bird. Why, I just can't get that man to sit down and relax for one minute. He's always doing some job or fixing some broken-down thing." She cupped her hands around her mouth and yelled back up at him, "There's a fresh pot of coffee just perked and a new batch of my potato doughnuts out of the fryer. You all come on in now." She wiped her hands on her apron, and then wagged a finger up at him. "And get down from there before you break your neck."

Auntie, Lizzie and Crystal, one of the quiet young girls who had been at supper, bustled around the large farm kitchen that morning, baking cookies and rolling out pie dough. Although I offered to help, Auntie waved me away, insisting she had enough people in the kitchen.

When I asked her if Andy had been down for breakfast yet, Auntie threw up her hands and laughed. "Child, there's not been a peep from either of them boys yet. I 'spect they're still sleeping. Why don't you wander into town and look around?"

I was anxious to explore, so I grabbed my purse and headed for the Skylark. Armed with a current map of Bridgeport, along with the 1900 map I'd sketched from Miss Randolph's book (which I didn't want to take away from Auntie's house), marking places of interest in Whitehead's life, I headed north to Bridgeport. At the Main Street exit, I cruised slowly through the city, turning right at the State Street light, then right again towards Pine Street, where Gustave Whitehead had lived. Signs pointed towards the old Barnum and Bailey Winter Quarters situated just down the street from Whitehead's first home. According to Stella Randolph's book, Whitehead had made a number of experimental flights from those very grounds.

Pulling up to the curb, I read the plaque describing the circus site. The old railroad tracks glinted in the morning sun, as they passed by the Winter Quarters. Huge shade trees lined the street giving the grassy lawn a park-like appearance. A few people strolled with dogs on leashes and one young woman held two small boys by their hands while a third little girl danced around them as they walked. A man threw a Frisbee hard for an eager border collie. But for the most part, the open area was deserted. I wrinkled my nose at the salty, fishy breeze that tugged at my jacket and skirt.

Pine Street was only a couple of blocks away. Turning from Howard Street, onto Pine, I parked at the curb, got out. A couple of boys on bicycles sped by, but otherwise the neighborhood was quiet. A small plaque situated in front of 241 Pine declared Gustave Whitehead the Connecticut Father of Aviation. At least someone recognized his achievements.

A man's voice from behind caught me by surprise. "Beautiful day, isn't it?"

I fumbled the sketched map in my hands, trying to catch it as it floated to the ground. Looking back, I recognized the man from the first morning of my trip and last night in the car. His creepy smile almost took my breath away as he stood towering over me by at least a foot. He shook his head and clucked his tongue as if I were a bad girl for dropping the map, then bent over to retrieve it.

"You!" I yelled. "Who are you? What do you want?"

He glanced at the paper in his hand. "Ah, I see you're still interested in that Whitehead fraud. What a waste of time." He wadded up the sheet with one hand. "There are more interesting things to see in this city than this."

"What I do is none of your business," I snapped. "Just give that paperback and leave me alone. Besides, why do you care?"

"Well, I personally don't, but I've been hired to convince you to give up this crazy Whitehead search. You're not related to him, so why are you doing this?" The man held up the crumpled map in the palm of his hand, just out of my reach.

Although I eyed it, I folded my arms across my chest and glared at him. "Hired? Who do you work for?" The quiver in my voice destroyed any attempt at boldness.

He laughed and took a step closer, stuffing the balled up map into his coat pocket. "What makes you think this Whitehead guy actually flew any airplanes at all? There is no proof, you know. No photographs, no records. Why, no one's ever found any of his planes at all. It's all just a big hoax."

I glowered at him. "A hoax! No way. Lots of witnesses signed affidavits saying they saw him fly. What more proof do you want? There probably are pictures, somewhere, in someone's attic. And how can you say that his planes have never survived, just because they've not been found yet."

As I turned away from him, he grabbed my shoulders and turned me around to face him. "Now you listen to me."

"Get your hands off of me!" I attempted to pull away, but his fingers dug in.

"You forget it. You just leave it alone, you hear? I'd hate to see your little colored friends as victims of a sudden house fire. Or---"

"What's going on here?" demanded a gruff voice behind me.

The man glanced over my shoulder, a smile creeping onto his face as his grip loosened. I pulled away, smoothing my skirt with quivering hands.

A towering policeman, with graying sideburns and salt-and-pepper curls peeking out from underneath his cap, stared down at us. His brown eyes bored into the man while the bushy, gray mustache twitched. He looked at me. "Is he bothering you, Miss?"

"Yes, he is. He's been following me and just now he threatened me. I want him arrested." I grabbed my shoulder bag with a white-knuckled grip.

The man smirked at me as he stepped close to the policeman. "Can I have a word with you?" He tried to put his arm up around the officer, who brushed it away as they walked together, down the block. I started after them, anxious to find out what this man's story was.

The officer stopped me. "Please wait there for one second, Miss."

He stood there with his Billy club out, gently tapping it on the palm of his hand. The man smiled and talked fast while reaching into his hip pocket and flashing some kind of identification inside his wallet. With a brief nod of his head, the policeman turned back to me while the stranger hurried off to his car.

"I'm sorry if he bothered you, Miss. But my hands are tied. He is a government man and he didn't actually hurt you, did he? He claimed he didn't threaten you. He said you were simply overreacting and when you had time to think about it, you'd see the error of your ways." The officer paused and looked at the man's departing vehicle, "Whatever that means."

The policeman introduced himself as Thatcher Cook and wrote his phone number and name down on a slip of paper for me. "Call if that man persists in following or threatening you."

I thanked the policeman and watched him stroll around the corner and down the street. *The government! Why would they be interested in Gustave Whitehead? Why didn't the guy tell me he was with the feds? Maybe I've stumbled onto something big. I'll have to tell Andy about the fire threat so he can be on the lookout, in case the guy shows up again. After looking into that man's cold eyes, I know he is capable of carrying out such a horrendous act.*

After a final glance at the modest house where Whitehead had lived, I returned to my car and headed back towards Fairfield. Since I'd practically memorized the map from Randolph's book, I realized Auntie's house was probably close to Whitehead's last residence up on Tunix Hill. *I'll have to ask about that address.*

****

Later that morning, when I returned and entered my room, there was the Whitehead book sitting in the middle of my bed. *How strange. I'm sure I left it in the barn when I went to help Uncle Henry with the ladder. He must have found it.* As I picked up the book, it flipped opened to a folded, brown scrap of newspaper. I lay the paper aside, smiling at the photograph on the page of Gustave Whitehead leaning against his "airplane #21," holding one of the motors he had developed. The caption read, "Witnesses reported a flight by #21 on August 14, 1901, 28 months before the first flight of the Wright brothers." I was about to close the book when I noticed the neatly clipped, brittle rectangle of newspaper that I'd laid aside. When I unfolded it, the bold Bridgeport Sunday Herald banner leaped out.

Not another old newspaper article. Careful not to rip it, I unfolded it and spread it out on the bed. Dated 1911, it told of an entire Fairfield family that had been found dead in their home. Two young boys, one having been shot and one with a broken neck were laid out in an upstairs bedroom and down the hall were the parents' bodies, dead from gunshot wounds, probably suicide, after killing their own children. How horrible. There was something familiar about the family's address, though. I reached for my purse and pulled out the slip of paper with the directions to Auntie's house that Andy had given me. My heart raced as I opened the note. 28028 Tabitha Lane, Fairfield. *This was it. This was the place of those dreadful deaths.*

Chapter Nine

Ghosts

"Why?" I said as I clutched the frail article in my hand. In the barn's dimness, I squinted at Uncle Henry bent over his workbench, pounding nails into an old weather-beaten birdhouse. A streak of sunlight from the window in the loft sliced across the bench.

Uncle Henry straightened up and looked at me, his voice quiet. "Spirits live here. You best not stay."

I waved the article at him, my voice harsher than intended. "Oh, I don't believe in ghosts. Why is your family living in this place anyway? How could you live in a house where parents murdered their own children?"

"They did not kill their boys," he said simply. Then he raised his hammer and in one stroke, whacked another nail flush with the wood.

"What? How would you know, unless---?"

"I saw the boys hurt by a group of white men with guns one night. The men came back the next morning and there was gunfire in the house, but I don't believe Mr. Stromberg shot himself or his missus. He wouldn't do that." He put down his hammer and picked up a square of sandpaper.

I felt weak at the knees. "Men? What men? Did you tell the police?"

Uncle Henry shook his head. "Nobody believes what a nigger boy says."

Tears welled up but I refused to blink as I watched this old man.

"T'was a long time ago," he grunted, turning the wooden birdhouse over and smoothing a corner with the sandpaper.

Perched on the edge of a straw bale beside the workbench, I leaned forward. "So, why are you here?"

"This is about the only home I've ever known. I worked here as a stable boy during most of my childhood and bought the place thirty years later."

I couldn't help interrupting. "But how and why?"

Henry looked at me hard, and then shook his head. "Been through a war and worked all kinds of jobs across this country. Saved my money." He looked up and around the big room. "Besides, nobody else wanted it because they say it's haunted. Who would want a farm where they couldn't use the barn?"

"Ghosts?" I whispered. "Here?"

He laughed out loud. Then he quit abruptly and his eyes darkened. "You know, the next day, Mr. Stromberg told me the boys were dead. Only the boys' spirits are still here in the barn. But they don't bother me none," he told me, smiling at my wide-eyed gaze. "They were only young boys anyway. What harm can they do?"

A rustling of straw overhead drew their attention to the loft. I clamped my hand over my mouth to keep from screaming.

"Probably just a cat," he declared, smiling. "Those boys won't bother you at all, long as their secret remain undisturbed."

84

"Secret? What secret?"

"There's Andy now." Uncle Henry turned back to his workbench and tidied up the small cans of paint he'd used on the weather-vane.

Andy strolled in and stood with his hands in his pockets with a bemused smile. "There you are," he said. "Been wondering where you disappeared to. Auntie told me to find you and see if you wanted any lunch."

"Oh, hi Andy." I glanced at my watch. "I guess it is that time. I just got back from Bridgeport and was out here looking for the book I'd left in the barn earlier. Uncle Henry was telling me about...about the old days when he worked here as a stable boy."

"Really," said Andy, looking from Uncle Henry to me and back again.

Uncle Henry eyed him for a moment before giving a quick nod then turning back to his painting job. Andy looked at me and motioned towards the house.

"Come on. Auntie has some of her famous potato donuts just out of the fryer. You never tasted anything as good as them, believe you me! You too, Uncle Henry, you'd better come in before they're all gone."

A board creaked somewhere in the rafters above their heads and bits of straw tumbled lazily to the ground. I jumped with a brief squeal. Uncle Henry half smiling, as I backed cautiously out the barn door with Andy.

The kitchen smelled wonderful. Rows of steaming donuts, on wire racks, lined the counter next to the oven. Lizzie dipped each one into a large bowl of powdered sugar before putting them on the big ceramic platter.

85

"Now you kids leave at least two of those for your Uncle when he comes in," ordered Auntie. She stacked the last plate in the drainer and pulled the plug on the sudsy sink water. "I've got some ham sandwiches here for your lunch." Then she turned towards me, drying her hands on her flowered apron. "So, Lorie, how was your trip to town this morning?"

"It was..." All of their eager faces watched. "Interesting." Leaving out the meeting with the government man, I simply said, "I saw the house where Gustave Whitehead first lived in Bridgeport and was going to check out the house on Tunix Hill but wasn't sure exactly where it was. It's near here, isn't it?"

"Why, it's just up the road about half a mile. It's right up on the top of the hill surrounded by large trees. You can't miss it," said Auntie.

"Maybe this afternoon I'll head over there," I said. "Say, would it be OK if I took these last two donuts out to Uncle Henry? He's really busy with that birdhouse."

"Certainly, child. I'll fix Daddy some nice warm coffee you can take out too, if you think you can carry it all." She heaped sugar and cream in a large ceramic mug that looked like a bear, and then filled it from the percolator and stirred it vigorously before handing it to me.

With the donuts double-wrapped in napkins in one hand and the steaming mug in the other, I left Andy chatting with his aunt and returned to the barn. The instant I slid open the oversized door and slipped between the narrow gap, Uncle Henry looked up briefly from his workbench before going back to painting the light blue birdhouse with a thin, bright-red trim.

"Didn't want you to miss out on these delicious donuts. So I brought some out here. Auntie sent a mug of coffee too," I said, setting the food on the empty end of the bench. I cleared my throat. "Say, did you ever actually see Gustave Whitehead fly his plane?"

Uncle Henry looked up this time and stared at me a moment before answering. "Many times."

"No kidding. Did he really fly successfully before the Wright Brothers?"

"Yes."

"If I run up and get my tape recorder, would you be willing to tell me about those flights?" I asked. "I'm trying to write that article about Mr. Whitehead and I sure could use your eyewitness account."

"You think anyone will believe me?" asked Uncle Henry, laying down his paint brush. "After all, I'm only a colored man."

"How about if I don't mention that part. No one will know, will they?" I said. "Be right back, OK?"

I raced out of the barn and taking two steps at a time burst into my upstairs room. *This is my big chance. If I can just get Uncle Henry to talk about those flights, I know the article will be a huge success. And it might even change the course of history!* With the tape recorder tucked under my arm, along with the Stella Randolph book, I ran all the way back out and slipped through the still open barn door.

I huffed and puffed, waiting for my eyes to adjust to the murky light inside. The workbench loomed beneath the loft with the freshly painted birdhouse propped up on one edge. The donuts and coffee were still on the far end, right where I'd left them.

"Uncle Henry?" I laid the tape recorder next to the food.

87

All was silent.

"Uncle Henry!" I yelled louder, stepping back at the sound of my echoed voice. A scraping sound came from the loft above. My heart thumped wildly in my chest. "Are you up there?"

I stood at the base of the loft ladder, my mouth dry, trying to get the courage to climb up, when I heard the barn's large sliding door closing. I spun around and screamed, "No!"

Dashing for the door, I grabbed a shovel propped up against a post and jammed it in the opening only a moment before it completely shut. The door creaked to a halt. Wedged open, there was plenty of room for me to slide my fingers in to pull it open. I heaved with everything I had but couldn't move it, even sitting with my foot braced against the shovel handle.

It's hopeless. Someone must be outside holding it shut. I stood up and peered through the small opening. Most of the yard and house were visible, but no one seemed to be out there. I held my breath and listened. Silence. *Why did the door close? Who would want to shut me in the barn? And where is Uncle Henry? Maybe if I yell, someone in the house will hear me.* This time when I peered through the opening, there was someone walking slowly towards me from around the edge of the house. I squinted, trying to see who it was. *Oh my God! The government man from town! He's coming towards the barn toting a pail.*

I stumbled backwards away from the door, and dashed to Uncle Henry's workbench, squatting down behind it. The sliding door groaned as the man tried to open it. When he couldn't, there was silence for an instant followed by several thuds as if he were kicking it. I couldn't breathe. The shovel clattered to the floor, but the door didn't budge.

88

"Hey, you in there. Open up," he said, his fingers slipping through the gap. "I just want to ask you a question." He heaved and grunted, but the door didn't move any further.

I sat as still as possible behind the bench, while the man cursed, yelled and kicked at the door. *Hopefully they'll hear all the yelling in the house and come outside. Yell louder, jerk!*

"Open up in there! Hey I just want to talk to you," he bellowed. "Damn it, open up!"

Abruptly, the door slammed all the way shut. He hadn't had time to pull his hands back and screamed. I heard people yelling in the yard. Burlus' and Andy's voices rose above the rest.

"I've got him, Andy," yelled Burlus. "Get into the barn and find some rope. We're going to tie this sucker up before we call the cops."

"You've got that right," agreed Andy.

Light burst into the barn when the door slid open. Andy seemed to have opened it with no effort whatsoever.

"Lorie!" he exclaimed when he saw me rise from behind the workbench. "What in the world are you doing in here?"

"Thank God you came. There's a whole lot of rope here on the shelf behind me." I handed him the coil. "You be sure to tie him up good."

"Are you all right?"

"I'm fine...now."

"Boy, you sure did a great job slamming that door shut on his hands. I think you broke a couple fingers. You really caught him good," said Andy. "Did you know he has a bucket of gasoline soaked rags? Looks like he meant to burn the place down."

"I'm not surprised. But I didn't close the door on him. I was trapped in here and was trying to get out when he came up and tried to get in. I ran back behind this bench and hid, hoping he wouldn't find me. The door just sort of shut by itself. I don't know how, though."

"Now, don't joke with me. There's no way that door could shut by itself," said Andy. "It sure wasn't stuck now when I opened it."

It was a relief to leave the barn and walk out into the sunlight. Burlus had the situation well in hand and was getting all kinds of help from Auntie, Uncle Luther and the girls as he tied up the man. Andy and I were still discussing the mystery of the stuck door when Uncle Henry emerged from the house and walked towards them. As I explained to him what had happened, he chuckled.

"What's so funny?" I demanded, not finding the situation the least bit humorous.

Uncle Henry looked me straight in the eye. "Them boys like you. If they didn't, you'd have been the one with the broken fingers instead of that scum. They were protecting you...and their secret. Count yourself lucky."

Andy looked totally confused. "What secret? What boys?"

I looked at Uncle Henry. "The boys?"

Uncle Henry nodded, clearly amused. In fact, it was the first time I'd actually seen him happy. I turned towards a puzzled Andy. "I'll explain everything to you in the house."

Chapter Ten

Flight

I dug in my purse and pulled out the card the policeman had given me in town earlier. Thatcher Cook. *What an odd name, but what a nice man.* After I made the call to Officer Cook, I pulled Andy aside and told him about my trip to Bridgeport that morning and the threats the man had made.

"But, why?" asked Andy. "What did Gustave Whitehead ever do to him? And why is the government interested in all this? Come on, we're going out and talk to that guy before the police get here."

"I don't think that will do any good. We'd better let the police handle him. It'll be a relief to have him put behind bars while I'm here," I said. "The person I need to talk to is Uncle Henry."

Officer Cook and two other policemen thoroughly questioned me, while they removed the ropes that bound the man. Then they cuffed him and took him away. He turned and winked at me before he climbed into the police car. *He sure is a cocky jerk. Hope they put him away for good!*

Andy seemed restless next to me, as the police car rolled down the driveway. "Listen, I need to run some errands for Auntie. Let me know how it goes with Uncle Henry."

I shrugged and shook my head as I watched him leave. *I can't believe he doesn't want to be there when I talk to Uncle.* I headed for the barn.

This time, when I entered, Uncle Henry was putting the finishing touches on the birdhouse. The empty donut

91

napkin was folded neatly beside his half mug of coffee and he softly whistled through his teeth, just the way my grandfather used to. As I approached, he stopped and looked up.

I set the cassette player on the end of the workbench plank, then reached over and pushed the Play/Record button.

Just take a deep breath and relax. "So, you actually saw Gustave Whitehead fly?"

He didn't look up but nodded, dipping his thin paintbrush in a jar of black paint.

"Were you there when he made the August, 1901 flight that was covered by the newspaper?"

He looked up and straight into my eyes. "Who do you think helped push the plane out to Lordship Manor that morning? Junius and I and some older fellows took it out there a little before dawn. Mr. Whitehead flew for about a half mile for the first flight and later in the afternoon, he made an even longer one. One of the men watching said it was close to a mile and a half."

"What?" I exclaimed. "He made more than one flight that day?"

"Sure did." His voice seemed to get softer. "Let me think---three, no four flights that day. They only mentioned the first one in the newspaper articles, though. But I was there."

I couldn't believe my ears. "You mean there were two articles? I saw the one from the New York Herald. What paper was the other article in?"

He pulled at his chin in thought. "I believe it was in the Boston Transcript, if I recall correctly. You'd have to look it up if there are any records left from that paper.

"Mr. Whitehead must have been so excited with two newspaper articles and more than one successful flight in one day!"

"Well, no. He was never satisfied with his flights. Instead, he complained that the steering or take-off or something wasn't just right. Oh, he was mighty pleased he didn't damage Number 21, but he didn't do any celebrating," insisted Uncle Henry. He rinsed his paint brush. "You have to remember that the Barnum and Bailey Circus wintered in Bridgeport, so unusual things were commonplace around here. But, I did hear him yell to his misses when we all got back to the house, 'Mama, we went up!'"

"Wow. That must have been something to see."

"We boys sure whooped and hollered each time he left the ground and came down in one piece," chuckled Uncle Henry. "But you know, we helped him many times with his flying machines. Sometimes the practice flights went good but then one time we saw one of his planes go up in flames. Sometimes they just crashed when they landed."

I glance over at the cassette recorder, making sure it was still running. "How come people don't believe he flew at all? I don't understand."

Uncle Henry gathered all of his paintbrushes together and poured turpentine into a small, dented, metal bucket. "Nobody took flying as a serious thing back then. I think most people thought it was some kind of stunt or trick. Some even thought it was the work of the devil. You know like---'If God had intended man to fly, he would have given him wings' sort of thing," he mused. "Besides, a lot of people thought Mr. Whitehead was off in the head. That's why they called him 'Crazy Whitehead.'"

93

"Really? They called him that to his face? Didn't it make him angry?"

"Nah, he just laughed it off. He didn't care what folks said. He was used to it. But we boys saw him fly and we knew he wasn't crazy at all. He was just real smart." He took each of the brushes and flicked them against a post to knock the moisture off.

"How come no one took pictures of him flying?" I asked.

"Well now, I think someone may have when he made that longer flight a year or so later. It was in January of 1902. I saw someone with a camera then, but I couldn't be sure if he got anything. You see, back then, those cameras were big and heavy, and hard to manage, so regular folks didn't have one. It was really hard to take pictures of things that moved too. Not like today." He replaced the lids on all of his paint jars except on with black paint.

"So what happened to all of Mr. Whiteheads stuff when he died?" I asked.

"I don't rightly know. I left the area before he passed on," replied Uncle Henry, placing a big hook through the eyelet on the top of the birdhouse. "I do know that year before he died, he got himself in some kind of legal trouble and a bunch of men came and took all of his tools, engines, and flying stuff away from him. But I hear tell he did actually build some engines after that time. He even sold some to a man who made airplanes for the mail service."

"They took everything away? But what do you suppose they did with it?"

Uncle Henry smiled and looked me straight in the eye. "Now, if I was to answer that, those young boys who died here might get angry. We don't want that, now, do we?"

I gawked at him. "You know, don't you? You can't keep a secret like that. The world deserves to know!"

"Do they?" Above his head, Uncle Henry fastened a metal wire between two close posts, twisting the ends to make it taut.

"Mr. Whitehead should get some credit for all he's done for flying. Why, if it could be proven that he flew two whole years before the Wright Brothers, that fact could change history! Wouldn't you like to see Mr. Whitehead be named the 'Father of Aviation' instead of the Wrights? I could do that if you would tell me where his flying equipment is. If I could present that to the Smithsonian with hard proof that he flew successfully, they'd have to listen."

"Now what makes you think just finding some of his stuff would be proof that he actually flew?" he asked, as he hooked the birdhouse on the wire to dry. He picked out a small clean brush and dipping it in the black paint, daubed at the underside, as it hung.

"Well, maybe there are some pictures or actual plans of the planes that would prove that---" I started.

"...and maybe not."

"If you show me where it is, I promise I won't say a word to anyone if there isn't any actual proof."

Uncle Henry stopped and looked at the barn door as it slid open.

Burlus poked his head through. "Hey, Lorie. There's a phone call for you. I think it's that cop who was just here."

Rats! Just when I was about to get Uncle Henry to tell me his secret! I followed Burlus into the house and picked up the receiver from the kitchen counter. "Hello, this is Lorie."

"Thatcher Cook here again. I had just gotten that fellow, Jeb Bracken, from your farm and locked him up when I got a call from my Captain to let him go. He said that since Bracken didn't actually set fire to your barn, there was really no crime committed. I tried to tell him there was intent, but he wouldn't listen. As Bracken walked out, I warned him not to go near your place, but he just smiled at me. I didn't want to let him go, but I had to." His Irish accent was more pronounced than it had been in town. "I figured you'd like to know. If you hear from that scoundrel or even see him, call me. I'll personally take care of him the next time."

"I'll keep my eyes open for him." Then I added, "Oh, and thank you, Officer Cook."

"That sounds so formal. I'd be honored if you'd call me Thatcher, like all my friends do," he said.

I smiled. "Thanks, Thatcher."

"All part of the job, Lorie."

When I hung up, Andy asked, "Why did he call? Don't tell me they let that guy go already."

"Afraid so," I replied. "He must have had some pretty heavy connections to get him off that fast."

"Do you think he'll come back?"

"I hope not."

****

Midafternoon, Andy and I walked about a mile down the country road to Gustave Whitehead's last residence. Still there, the Tunix Hill place looked like someone had

96

added extra rooms to the original house along with a couple of metal sheds. People appeared to be living in it, so we didn't go into the yard, but stayed at the road. The old peach trees in the orchard by the house had sprouted buds and a fenced-off area looked freshly tilled for a garden. *Spring is definitely here.*

The walk was very relaxing and I was glad we had decided not to take the car. Only a few vehicles passed by. We barely crossed the narrow road to head for home when a dark sedan whizzed by. Since it was going the same direction as us, we stepped off the pavement onto the gravel shoulder. It squealed to a stop a few yards ahead, and then backed up slowly until it was even with us. Andy stepped between the car and me.

The driver, a cap pulled low over his eyes, rolled down his window and poked his head out. "Excuse me. Could you direct me to this address?"

He waved piece of paper at Andy, who stepped over to the car and glanced down at it. "Is that number a three or an eight?"

The man's left hand, which dangled down the side of the car, reached out and grabbed the front of Andy's shirt. Pulling him in close, he punched Andy square in the face. I stood frozen to my spot as Andy's body sagged to the ground. A man sprang from the passenger's seat, darted around the car and grabbed me around the waist. I gasped, recognizing the man as Jeb Bracken, then pulled back, screaming and kicking. Even though I beat at him with my fists, he continued to stuff me into the backseat of the car and slam the door. I reached for the door-handle to open the door, but there was no handle. *It has been removed!* I lunged across at the other door, but it too was missing its handle. *There is no escape!* Bracken had jumped back into the front passenger's side and grinned back at me through a window that separated the front from the back, like a police car.

"You!" I yelled at him, pounding on the glass. "What are you doing here? Why did you hurt Andy and where are you taking me?" The driver threw the car into gear and everyone jerked back in their seats as he squealed away down the road.

"Just settle down, sweetheart," said Bracken. "We have a few questions to ask you. If you cooperate, you'll be back with your colored boyfriend by dark."

Chapter Eleven

Questions

I sat tall in my seat, looking out the window. *I have to get someone's attention. It's obvious I can't escape from this car until it stopped, with no door handles on the backseat doors. What does Jeb Bracken and the mysterious driver want with me? How could they hurt Andy and then just leave him there? Where are they taking me?* I stared out the window. My sweaty hand trembled as I brushed away a tear. The car careened around a sharp curve and threw me across the seat. I could feel Bracken watching me even though I refused to look at him.

Heading into Bridgeport, taking side streets, the car wound through town until it reached the waterfront. The late afternoon sun threw long shadows on a cluster of tents still on the beach from the Farmers' Market earlier in the day. Unfortunately, the car didn't stop but continued past sparse crowds, outdoor cafes, and colorful stands heading towards the far side of the marina.

Two and three-story, run-down warehouses perched like ghost towns on the water's edge on pilings jutting out from the shore, with the ocean lapping onto the sand beneath them. The car swerved around a small group of colorful Vietnam War protesters walking in the same direction, carrying peace signs. A skinny, bearded, long-haired, guy in an orange tie-dye shirt had a folk guitar slung over his shoulder. When the group yelled at the car as it passed, I pressed my face to the window and waved frantically to them. The guy with the guitar noticed and gave me two thumbs up as the car sped by.

A block later, the sedan jerked to a halt in front of a weathered two-story building with "Billingstone Shipping"

99

stenciled across two large sliding wooden doors, much like the ones on Auntie's barn.

The driver nodded towards me as he spoke to Jeb Bracken. "Take her inside and get her settled. I got another appointment. Be back later tonight with the boss." Then he added, "And for God's sake, don't draw any attention to yourselves."

"Yeah, right," said Jeb.

The driver tapped his fingers on the steering wheel as if he was annoyed that he had to wait. Jeb flung open the car door and leaped out. Before I knew what was happening, he threw open the back door, reached in and yanked my arm, dragging me out. "Don't fight me."

"Ow! You're hurting me," I shouted, trying to pull away. He drew out a gun tucked in his waistband and jabbed it into my lower back, shoving me ahead of him. The faint strains of a strumming guitar danced in the air. He glanced back at the crowd of protesters who were still several blocks back. Then, turning back, he shoved the revolver harder into my back, pointing towards a door beside the huge wooden one.

When I stopped abruptly at the door, Jeb grunted and stumbled into me. I back peddled to keep from falling and inadvertently tromped down on his foot. He swore. "Hey, watch where you're going!" Flecks of gray peeled paint drifted to the ground as he reached around me to open the door.

Inside, the air, musty and dank, stacked crates towered to the ceiling all along the left and back walls, many almost blocking the few windows that let in splotches of light. To the right, a metal stairway ascended towards a glass-enclosed room on the second floor. As he shoved me forward towards the stairs, a rat scurried across the path

100

and disappeared among the wooden crates. I paused and shivered.

Jeb prodded me in the back. "Up the stairs."

Cold and slippery under my hand, I hung on tightly to the pipe handrail. The stairs clattered with each step. They reminded me of old iron fire escapes on the outsides of high-rises that I'd climbed as a kid. *Nobody's going to sneak up these noisy steps or down them either.* When we got to the top, Jeb reached around me and unlatched the door. Shoving me inside, he hit the light-switch. A fluorescent light blinked on for a moment then snapped off.

"Damn power's gone off again," Jeb growled. He turned and slammed the door shut behind him, blocking out what little light the open door had provided. I stumbled into a swivel desk chair that had rolled away from the desk. "You just sit tight there while I find the candle."

Instead, I lunged towards his voice, hoping to knock the gun away in the dark. We collided and I grabbed his extended arm. He knocked me to the floor. My head bounced off the wooden planks, and through the pain everything swirled round and round. I lay still, trying to focus when the unmistakable snap of a lighter broke the quiet. A candle flickered, throwing sparse light and confusing shadows. My lip hurt and when I reached to touch it, my hand came away bloody. My gaze fixed on a lone light surrounded by red, blue, green and yellow streams of wax cascading down the sides of an old wine bottle, obliterating the brand label. The light glinted off the ceiling and walls as Jeb set the candle on a desk behind me. I jerked when I realized he was kneeling beside me as I lay on the floor. In his hand was a roll of duct tape. "I can see you're going to be difficult, so I'll have to subdue you. Don't fight me or I'll hit you harder."

He bound my hands with strips of duct tape, and then jerked me to my feet. No sooner had I regained balance than he pushed me into the swivel desk chair. Then with several passes with the tape, he attached my feet to the chair's metal base.

"Now, I have a few questions for you. If you tell the truth, I'll let you go. But if you lie or play games with me..." He retrieved the gun from the floor and slapped it down on the desk. Picking up the candle, he held the flame so close to my face that the heat stung my cheeks. "Let me put it this way---I love everything about fire: how it looks, how it smells, and especially how it makes people talk." He waved the candle slowly in front of me, nearly catching my hair on fire, and grinned. "And I'm very good with it."

I recoiled from the flame. "What do you want from me? I can't imagine anything I know that would be of interest to you. You do know that kidnapping is a felony, don't you?"

He laughed. "I'm not kidnapping you. I don't want any money. I just want answers, so I'm only detaining you for a while. I need to know what you know about Gustave Whitehead."

I vigorously shook my head. "I don't know what you're talking about."

With a tight-lipped smile, he reached out and touched my face; his sweaty fingers passing slowly over my nose, cheeks and jawbone, wiping away a trail of blood from my swollen lip. I leaned back, trying to avoid his hand. "No, please stop. Don't."

"But you are too luscious," he whispered, bringing the candle closer to my chin. His hand didn't stop at my neck, but crept down, tracing the outline of my breasts, firmly squeezing each as it passed. "Stop! Please don't!" I screamed. "Just let me go. God, let me go!" I tried to squirm away and felt the chair move with each thrust.

He slapped me hard. "Your screaming will do no good. Nobody can hear it. Shut up or I swear I'll set you on fire!"

Then he held his foot on the metal chair base to keep the chair still and no matter how hard I tried to free my legs or push away, I couldn't. Sobbing and closing my eyes, I hoped all of this was just a nightmare and I'd wake up back at Andy's house. *If I can just quit shaking.* My heart beat so fast, I thought it would jump from my chest. Then, abruptly, he let go of me. I opened my eyes. Tears blurred my vision and dripped inside the collar of my blouse.

A clatter came from below followed by a pounding on the entrance door. He turned towards the sound and then back to me. "I can't trust you to keep quiet, can I?"

I sat open-mouthed, too scared to reply or even nod. He glanced quickly around the room and snatched an old dirty rag from a hook on the wall. "No! Please, no!" I shook my head violently as he forced the oily cloth into my mouth.

He snatched up his gun just as a beam of light appeared downstairs at the outside entrance. The brightness from the open door was replaced by the silhouette of a tall, shaggy figure.

"Hey, anybody here?" asked a deep voice.

The candle flickered and danced as Jeb ran through the office door onto the landing. When the figure stepped through the doorway, I saw it was the tie-dye hippie with the guitar that we'd passed on the street. He apparently had spotted Jeb on the stairs because he yelled and pointed, "You there --- we need to use a john. One of the girls is really sick, man."

"What do you think this is? A public toilet? You're trespassing on private property," Jeb growled. I couldn't see the hippie from where I sat. *He is probably standing in the shadows.* I wiggled myself towards the glass, jamming the chair against the window. Jeb's voice got louder. "Get out! And don't come back here again."

"Hey, cool it, man," said the hippie. "We don't want no trouble. All we need is a restroom. You must have one of those around here. Hey, why don't you turn on a light. It's awfully dark in here."

"Our breaker blew. Find someplace else. Now out!" Jeb ordered.

The shaggy man peered up to where I sat. I squirmed and pitched against the window with a thud.

"Hey, who's that up there in that room? I saw a girl come in here with you. George insists he heard a scream from inside here a few minutes ago. Is that her? Hey! What's going on here?"

"None of your business, hippy," snapped Jeb.

The guy suddenly put his hands up and stepped back a step. "Hey, dude, no need for guns. Don't do anything rash. There's a whole crowd of people just outside the door," he said. "You shoot me and you'll have to shoot all of them too."

Out of the shadows, Jeb dove towards the man, knocking him in the side of the head with his weapon. The man crumpled to the ground. Jeb glanced once more up at me before darting out the door. There was a slight commotion outside, then several people in tie-dye shirts and long beads began to trickle in through the open door. The shaggy guy lay in a heap on the floor while two young women hovered over him. He slowly sat up, and rubbing his head, looked up at me and pointed. A round, bald man and a frizzy-haired woman headed for the stairs.

When they reached me, the bald guy yanked the rag from my mouth and pulled out a pocket knife to cut the duct-taped bindings. "Hey, are you all right? That cut on your lip looks awful."

"I'm OK, but my hands are numb from the tight tape," I told him. "Did Jeb leave?"

"That horrible man ran out of here and up the street." The woman took the jackknife from the man and carefully sawed the tape binding my hands until it snapped. Then she continued cutting the rest of it off my legs and feet.

I was rubbing the red marks on my wrists when two young girls burst into the office. One of them, a tall, blond girl, asked, "Where's the john? I really need a john." The other one with a red headband and tight blue-jean cut-offs, collided with the desk, knocking the candle off the desk.

I nodded towards a closed door on the far side of the office. "It might be through there, but I don't know for sure."

They both bolted for the door and flung it open. "Finally!" the blond girl yelled. She ran in ahead, followed by the other girl, who slammed the door behind her.

The pungent smell of smoke filled the air. As I swiveled in the chair towards the desk, flames shot up from the wastebasket at its far end. The bald man and the woman leaped back. I jumped from my chair, looking around for anything to smother the fire.

"Hey, you girls get out of the john! There's a fire! Hurry!" shouted the bald man as he stripped off his tee shirt. He flung it at the spreading fire but rather than putting it out, flames licked up onto the shirt and he dropped it, pushing the other woman and me towards the stairs. The girls rushed from the bathroom as he yelled, "Come on. Let's get out of here!"

By the time all of us had clattered down the stairs and reached the outside door, the upstairs office was filled with flames and smoke. Glad to be away from the warehouse, I followed the crowd of protesters as they ran down the street. Two blocks later, as we rounded the corner towards the ocean, the group halted. Most of the group plopped onto the freshly mown lawn under a large oak tree. At the curb sat an old school bus covered with peace signs, multi-colored butterflies, and "Get out Vietnam," "Bring our soldiers home," "Down with War" signs.

I leaned against the tree and read the graffiti on the bus when the shaggy man approached, pressing a wet red bandana to the side of his head. "Hey, are you all right? How's that lip? That guy didn't do nothing to you, did he?"

"Oh, it's still a little sore, but it'll be fine," I said, touching my lip. "And no, he didn't have a chance, thanks to you. I hope you're OK. I don't know how to thank you, nor do I even know your name."

"My friends call me Shep. Hey, we're all brothers and sisters here."

"Well, thanks, Shep. I'm Lorie." I glanced off to the southwest at the smoke billowing up in the evening twilight. "Do you think we should try to call the fire department or something? I'd hate to have that fire spread too far."

Sirens sounded in the distance, getting louder by the minute. "Nope," said Shep. "Looks like someone has already done that. I wouldn't worry about it. There's hardly any wind today. Say, we're going to split from here. The place will be swimming with cops and we usually try to avoid them. Can we give you a lift somewhere?"

"Yes, I could sure use a ride," I said with a sigh. "It's been an awfully long day."

****

106

The yard at Auntie's farm appeared crowded, with Auntie's old pick-up, Burlus' white mustang, my Skylark, Uncle's beat-up Toyota and a black-and-white police car. The outside spotlight was so bright that it was hard to believe it was almost 8:00 at night. When I stepped inside the farmhouse, nobody noticed at first. Officer Cook, that nice policeman from Bridgeport, along with Andy's relatives sat around the dining table, all talking at the same time.

The stranger caught my eye instantly. A Spanish man with short, black, curly hair, dark eyes and a pencil-thin mustache, sat across from Auntie. He listened intently as she talked, waving her arms in the air as she always did when she was excited. He smiled at her antics, two dimples appearing on his cheeks. I thought he was the most handsome guy I'd ever seen. Then Auntie spotted me in the doorway and jumped up from her chair.

"Child! My goodness!" She ran and hugged me. "Are you all right? What's happened to you? Where have you been?"

Everyone stared. The stranger stood and bowed slightly, his eyes full of concern. "Lorie Drucker, I presume?" His accent was like melting chocolate, sweet and warm.

"Yes," I replied, exploring my lower lip wound with my tongue as everyone stared.

"We wondered what had happened to you. Are you all right?" asked the man.

I nodded rubbing my bruised wrists, while explaining how I'd been taken to a warehouse on the waterfront, where Jeb Bracken had forced me inside and duct-taped my hands and feet.

Auntie interrupted, "How did you ever escape that crazy man? Andy has been beside himself since he arrived back here at the house. He called the police and they came right out." Auntie took me by the hand and guided me towards the stranger. "This is Roberto Gutierrez. He's come all the way from Washington D.C. to investigate that Jeb Bracken person and wants to talk to you. Officer Cook suggested he come out to the house with him and since we have empty rooms upstairs, we've invited Roberto to stay."

I noticed his firm, warm handshake and dark, liquid eyes. "Nice to meet you, Mr. Gutierrez. But why would you want to talk to me? I don't know Jeb Bracken at all."

"Please, call me Rob. I work for an agency in Washington and we've been watching Bracken. How did you manage to escape from him?" He settled back in his chair and offered me the empty one beside him.

The chair scraped loudly as I pulled it out and sat down. A spicy scent drifted from Rob as he turned towards me. *What is that cologne he's wearing?* My heart pounded. All the eager faces at the table seemed full of questions. I took a deep breath. A tap on my shoulder made me jump.

Auntie stood there holding out a glass of ice water. "Here, take a sip of this. It will make your lip feel better and help you relax so you can tell us what happened."

Once I began, the words tumbled out almost faster than I could think. Questions bombarded me: "Did he hurt you?" "Did he get away?" "Will he come back here looking for you?"

Rob listened, saying nothing until I finished. But, as he opened his mouth to speak, the phone rang in the kitchen. Auntie slid back her chair to answer it. "What did Jeb Bracken want with you?" Rob asked in a quiet voice. Both his hands gripped his water glass on the table.

108

I shook my head. "I'm not sure. He didn't get much of a chance to ask me much before he was interrupted by my rescuers." Unsure if I could trust this good-looking stranger, I hesitated telling him the whole truth.

Auntie stood in the doorway to the kitchen and announced, "Lorie, there's a phone call for you. He said his name is Ben something."

Chapter Twelve

The Contract

Ben! Why are you calling here?

As if he could read my mind, Andy said, "I gave Ben our number here in case he had to contact us. Besides, he did ask for it."

I took the receiver from Auntie in the kitchen. "Ben? What's wrong?"

"Nothing's wrong. I dug up some information that I thought you might find helpful. By the way, how are you enjoying the trip? How's Andy?" he asked.

"Let me just say it's been anything but boring," I replied. "So, what exactly did you find?"

"Remember that contract the guy from the Museum was talking about? Well, since it hasn't come in your mail yet, I did a little research on my own," said Ben. "My Dad knows a man from his office whose niece works for some lawyers who worked for the Museum in Washington. I got the niece's phone number. And when I called her and asked about the contract, she whispered something very interesting; as if she were afraid someone might hear. She saw an agreement between the Wright Brothers' Estate and the Museum in the files at the law office. When she had mentioned it to a co-worker, he pulled her aside and told her if she valued her job, she'd forget she saw it. Of course, that made her more curious than ever."

"What happened? Did she get fired?" I asked.

"No. But she read the whole contract and managed to make a copy of part of it on the sly. She told me she did it for 'job security.'"

"So, what did the contract say?" I asked, barely above a whisper.

"Well, her copy came in the mail today," he said. I could almost see the grin on his face as he said it. "Listen to this part: '...it (referring to the 1903 flight of the Kittyhawk) was the first in the history of the world in which a machine carrying a man had raised itself by its own power into the air in free flight, had sailed forward on a level course without reduction of speed, and had finally landed without being wrecked.' Later it said, 'Neither the Smithsonian or its successors nor any museum or other agency, bureau or facilities, administered for the United States of America by the Smithsonian Institution or its successors, shall publish or permit to be displayed a statement or label in connection with or in respect of any aircraft model or design of earlier date than the Wright Aeroplane of 1903, claiming in effect that such aircraft was capable of carrying a man under its own power in controlled flight.'" Then he added, "It was signed in 1948."

"But that's not true," I insisted. "Uncle Henry saw Mr. Whitehead fly in 1901 and 1902. He was there during several flights!"

"The whole gist of this Contract was that if the Museum did not do as the Wrights said, the Kittyhawk would be taken away from them," Ben said. "Lorie, you've got to be careful with this thing. There are people out there who could really come down hard on you. Promise me you'll stay with Andy at all times. And don't spread it around too much that you're going to write an article about this."

My mind reeled as Ben talked on the other end. I wasn't really listening past that point, but was busy trying to figure out what I should do with this contract information.

111

"Listen, I have to go, Ben. Thanks for the call. Talk to you later." The line went dead. The dial tone buzzed in my ear. *Now I know why Jeb wants to question me. He was probably hired to find out what I've uncovered---but by whom? The Museum? The Wright estate? Well, I've found nothing yet, but I have a feeling I'm close to the proof needed to finish this article and expose the truth.*

"Well, what did he say?" asked Andy as I hung up the receiver.

"I'll tell you later," I whispered, walking back into the dining room.

****

Saturday morning sunlight poured into the windows of the barn glistening off the various cobwebs in the rafters. A tiger-striped cat darted from side to side as he raced across the hay-strewn floor after a mouse. Trotting with his catch proudly in his mouth, the tomcat disappeared behind a hay bale. Uncle Henry was back at his place behind the makeshift workbench.

"What do you know about the Wright Brothers?" I asked him as he put lids on his various paints, wiping each bottle clean before lining them up on the shelf behind the bench.

He stopped and looked at me. "They claim to be the first ones to fly a motorized airplane successfully in December of 1903."

"I mean, do you think they knew anything about Mr. Whitehead?" I asked.

"Well, I did see them one time when they came to Mr. Whitehead's shop. I remember asking Tony, (who was a

112

teenager and helped Mr. Whitehead build his motors) who those guys were that left Mr. Whitehead's shop. He told me they had introduced themselves as Wilbur and Orville Wright."

"Really? When was that?"

"Oh, I was five or six at the time but it happened sometime after the August, 1901 flight but before their Kittyhawk event in 1903. I just remember two men laughing and slapping each other on the back when they left Mr. Whitehead's shop. I asked Tony who those men were and what was so funny. Tony seemed mad and yelled at me, 'Those are the Wright Brothers from Ohio. They just took away the design that we've been working on for so long. Crazy gave it to them (that's what most folks called Mr. Whitehead). He just gave it to them.'"

"But why would he do that? Didn't he get patents for his airplane?"

Uncle Henry shook his head. "Mr. Whitehead never had enough money to get patents on his inventions," he replied. "Besides back then, nobody cared much about flying. Lot of folks thought it was the work of the devil and wouldn't even talk about it to no one. All Mr. Whitehead cared about was making his plane better. Probably never gave it a thought that anyone would want to steal any of his ideas."

"No patents at all?" I found it hard to believe I'd heard him right.

"Besides, Mr. Whitehead never became a U.S. citizen. He wanted to, but the Germans weren't liked much then and the couple of times he tried to get citizenship, he was turned down. You have to remember that was before World War I," explained Uncle Henry.

The barn door creaked behind me. Rob Gutierrez walked in carrying two steaming cups. Looking gorgeous in his tan slacks and multicolored sweater vest, his dark curly hair glistened as if he'd just gotten out of a shower.

"Beautiful morning, isn't it? Auntie said that I might find you out here. Brought you some black coffee," he said, handing me one of the cups.

"Thanks," I said.

"Do you want this other cup, Mr. Jackson?" Rob asked.

"No, sir." Uncle Henry turned towards the shelf, fiddling with the paint brushes and tools.

As he sipped the cup of coffee in his hand, Rob watched him for a moment before turning towards me. "I meant to ask you something last night, but I never got around to it." His smile was warm and his voice, like velvet, with that Spanish accent. "Exactly why did you come all the way out here to Bridgeport to Andy's family?"

I took several small sips from the cup while I thought. "Well, I met Andy at school and when he found out I wasn't planning anything for spring vacation, he invited me out here to meet his family."

"Are you and Andy, uh---" Rob began.

"No," I shot back. "He's just a friend." I took his arm and guided him back through the barn door into the bright sunlight. We walked up onto the front porch of the house and sat in two metal lawn chairs.

Rob shook his head. Then looking all around, he lowered his voice, "Why on earth would you choose to spend your whole spring break here with a colored family? You must get a lot of strange looks from people."

114

I remember what Ben said about not trusting people. "Well, Andy had told me all about his Uncle Henry and how he had grown up in this area and seen all kinds of stuff," I said, watching a chicken peck at the tire of one of the cars. Then I turned back to Rob. "Did you know that the Barnum and Bailey Circus wintered in Bridgeport around the turn of the century? I thought if I interviewed his uncle, I might be able to write an article about the history here, and maybe break into the magazine market."

Rob listened politely and smiled. "I see." He turned and looked at me, a slight smile on his lips. "What's that accent you have? You're not from around here, are you?"

I laughed; amused that someone with such a pronounced accent himself would think that I had an accent. "I live in Illinois but was raised in Michigan. Have you lived long in Washington D.C.?"

"Michigan! Why, I grew up there, until I went off to college. But in such a small town, you probably wouldn't know where it was."

"Oh, try me. I've been all over the state," I replied.

Rob hesitated. "Do you know where Paradise is?"

"On Lake Superior? But of course I do!" I chuckled. "We used to vacation up there every year."

"I don't believe it. I've never met anyone around here who even knew where that place was," he exclaimed with a grin. "I don't suppose you remember the General Store there?"

"You mean the one with that enormous moose head? I was sort of afraid of that thing when I was a kid," I said. "But I couldn't resist petting it each time we went in there."

Rob laughed. "I know what you mean! I worked for Mr. And Mrs. Berns for almost three years, part-time, when I was in High School." Memories from our childhoods tumbled out one after the other and I felt connected to this man, as if I'd known him for years.

When Uncle Henry strode across the yard to back door, we silently watched him. Rob stood and stretched his arms high above his head, turning his face directly into the blazing sun. "Interesting place, this farm. I don't suppose you know what happened here back in 1912."

I opened my mouth to respond, but Rob turned and jogging down the steps to the ground, disappeared around the side of the house. *What's with him? Why exactly is he here? And what do those deaths that occurred here have to do with Jeb Bracken?*

Chapter Thirteen

The Truth

That Saturday, I thought about all that had happened since I had arrived at Bridgeport. *All I wanted was to collect information for a simple article. But I still have nothing concrete.* I slowly shook my head, staring at the calendar on the wall. *Only a mere three days left before I have to return to Illinois.*

That night at dinner, I decided to find some answers.

The roast beef, mashed potatoes and gravy, and carrots and peas brought huge smiles to everyone as they settled at the table. After saying grace, the dishes were passed and everyone helped themselves. The air resonated with the clinking of silverware on the plates and goblets of water and milk. There wouldn't be a better time.

"Rob," I asked matter-of-factly, "what exactly do you know about the deaths that happened in this house back in 1912?"

A hush fell over the table. All eyes focused on Rob and me.

He laid his fork down and wiped his mouth with his napkin. "According to newspaper reports, the Stromberg family, who built this farm, was found dead inside the house. Apparently the father had murdered his two boys and his wife before shooting himself in the head. The rifle was found beside his body."

"No, that's not what happened," Uncle Henry said in a quiet voice from the opposite end of the table. He sat tall and stared ahead at no one in particular. It seemed like

117

everyone held their breath, waiting for him to continue. But he said no more.

Rob's voice was low and articulate. "How would you know that, sir?"

Uncle Henry related the same story he'd told me in the barn and everyone stared at him as though this was the first time they'd heard it. I watched Rob while he listened to Uncle Henry, but his lack of reaction mystified me. *He'd make a great poker player.*

"I saw the men come back the next day when I getting my stuff together. And there were shots in the house just before I left. Mr. Stromberg had told me the boys had both died the night before and that he would be leaving for a while," said Uncle Henry, taking a sip of water. "Don't know exactly what happened. Doesn't matter now, anyhow."

Rob's voice was almost a whisper. "What men? Why would they kill two young boys and then their parents?"

"Don't know. Didn't hang around to find out," Uncle said. Then he rose, laid the neatly folded napkin beside his plate, and walked through the kitchen, and outside. The screen door slammed in his wake like an exclamation point.

Rob turned towards Auntie. "So, how was it you came to own this place?"

Auntie shrugged. "Well, Daddy deeded it to me as a marriage present. You see, he bought it back in the '30's when the Strombergs' relatives, who still lived in Germany, finally put it up for sale." She stood up and began scraping and stacking the empty plates on top of hers. "Apparently no one seemed interested in owning a house where people had died so brutally. Knowing Daddy, he got a good price for it. Then, after Mother died, he didn't want to live here any longer, but refused to sell it to someone outside the family. He made me promise to keep it in the family, even if

118

I had to give it to a relative. Well, I couldn't turn down a free house." She gathered up the stack and glanced at Henry's empty seat. "This place has been home to me all my life, but in my heart, I know it still belongs to him." She stepped into the kitchen, setting her stack of dishes beside the sink. Then wiping her hands on the hand towel, she returned to the table.

"Did you know about the murders when you came to live here?" asked Rob.

"Well, I didn't know the details but I knew people had died here. When I asked Daddy about the strange noises in the barn, he just handed me an old newspaper clipping about the story. I know a lot of folks think this place is haunted, but really, I never heard anything here in the house," she replied, grabbing up a serving bowl and the bread basket. "Of course, I never go out to the barn. I send the kids out there to check the animals. That place gives me the shivers." She shuddered, before vanishing back into the kitchen.

Rob slowly shook his head. "I don't understand. If everyone died in the house, why are there only ghosts in the barn?"

Burlus laughed. "Aw, you don't really believe in ghosts, do you?"

Rob's expression was serious. "Yes, I do."

Burlus cleared his throat and tried not to smile as he continued eating. Andy didn't even look up as he scraped the last fork full from his plate. The girls, looking wide-eyed at each other, sat with their hands in their laps, food still on their plates.

I excused myself and stood up. "Well, I think I'll go outside for a walk." I picked up my plate and glass and carried them to the kitchen.

Chirping and croaking filled the cool evening air as I strolled across the side yard. The barn door was slid open just enough to slip inside. I stood for a moment while my eyes adjusted to the hazy moonlight filtering in through the windows and above from the open loft door.

"Uncle Henry?" My voice quivered. I cleared my throat and tried again, a little louder. "Uncle Henry? I know you're in here."

"Lorie. Come over here and hold this rope," came his voice. In the dimness, I could barely make out movement at the far end of the barn near one of the huge support beams. As I approached the rough-hewn post, I could just see his tall, lean figure hunkered over a thick rope with a mass of huge knots, wrapped around the post. His hand grasped a large hunting knife.

I was puzzled. "What are you doing?"

"The knots in this rope are too tight to untie, so I'm going to have to cut them. But first, I need to tie a second cord to this so we can control it if the main rope is accidentally cut." He handed me a coil of brand new line, which I took with both hands. Laying his knife down by the post, he grabbed the heavy rope well above the knots and fastened the new line to it. Then pulling the new line taut, he wound the end of it around a post supporting the loft a couple of time before tying it off. Then he nodded towards the open barn door. "You'd better stand back."

My gaze followed the old rope up into the dark rafters. The blackness seemed to go on forever. "What exactly is on the other end of that rope?"

With the new line clenched in his left hand, he ignored my question and began, with the other hand, to saw at the old knots with the knife. A screech pierced the silence. I jumped behind stacked straw bales and covered my head with my arms. A child's voice cried out, "You

120

promised! You promised!" echoing over and over. As the sound faded, I looked up to see Henry, having broken through several knots, still sawing away at another, as if he hadn't heard anything strange. I stood up, brushing bits of straw from my head and arms.

"Did you hear that? What was it?"

"Nothing. I'm almost through here. If you're going to stay in here, stand back under the loft, you hear?" Henry said. A loud snap came before he could sever the final knot, followed by a stutter of creaking wood from above. I backed under the loft, then craned my neck to peer up, half expecting something to come barreling through the darkness. But all that sifted down were pieces of dirt and straw and what appeared to be sawdust. The knots were all severed but the taut clothesline appeared to be holding whatever it was.

I opened my mouth to comment but a familiar voice from behind interrupted. "Go ahead, old man, cut it. Let's see what you've got stashed up there!"

Henry turned towards Jeb Bracken, who stood grinning just inside the open door. I gasped when I saw a flashlight in one hand and a pistol in the other, as I stepped back under the loft. *Did he see me? He seems to be watching Henry and peering up into the dark rafters.* Henry had stopped cutting.

"Come on, cut that line, or step aside and I'll shoot it down," Jeb ordered, waving the gun at the old man. Jeb traced the old rope with his flashlight beam up into the darkness above, which seemed to end in a dark blob at the peak of the roof. When Henry made no move to continue cutting, Jeb aimed the weapon at the old rope, just above the knot that joined the two cords, and pulled back the hammer.

121

Screeches and wailing filled the air before he could pull the trigger. With the gun and flashlight in his hands, Jeb struggled to cover his ears against the noise. Henry lurched towards Jeb, reaching for the pistol as he fell into him. Jeb beat on Henry with his flashlight, struggling to keep the gun while Henry fought to pull it away. They fell to the ground and rolled in my direction. When I stepped back to avoid them, the gun went off, the sound echoing throughout the barn. The two men lay still. I froze. Jeb struggled to move, throwing Henry's limp body aside as he sat up. "Damn fool," he muttered, brushing himself off and getting to his feet.

"No!" I shouted, dashing for the door opening.

"Stop right there," he ordered. Another shot rang out and I stopped in mid-step, turning back towards him.

Henry lay in a heap. Jeb stepped out around him and out from under the loft. Then, out of the darkness a chunk of wood fell, striking Jeb on the side of his head. He crumbled to the ground, the gun falling from his hand. I quickly stepped up and kicked the gun further away, then looked up into the dusky gloom. *That board must have been knocked loose from whatever was tied up there when Henry cut the rope.*

"Lorie! Are you OK? We heard gun shots!" Andy's anxious voice yelled, as the door slid open. Andy, Burlus and Rob raced inside.

I knelt down beside Henry. "I'm fine, but Uncle has been hit. Go call for help."

Burlus ran for the house. Andy and Rob huddled over Jeb, binding his hands behind his back with a small piece of rope.

When I pressed my fingers to the side of Uncle Henry's neck to check for a pulse, his eyes suddenly popped

122

open. I withdrew my hand and told him, "Help's on the way. Just lie still."

Blood seeped from the large wound in his side. His breathing was ragged. "You've got to promise me that you'll protect it," he whispered.

"Protect it? Protect what?" I leaned closer.

"The plane," was all he said before his eyes fluttered shut.

Chapter Fourteen

Proof

The plane? Is Uncle Henry referring to Whitehead's plane? But how is that possible? Has he have been hiding that plane in this barn all these years? What does the plane have to do with the boys dying? There has to be a connection.

Rob's voice startled me. "What did he say? How is he?"

Uncle Henry flinched when I pressed a clean paint rag over the wound. Tears crept down my cheeks. "We've got to stop this bleeding. When will the ambulance be here?"

Sirens screamed in the distance. "That sounds like them," said Andy. He knelt beside Uncle Henry and me. "Here, move aside. I'll do that. Boy, we could sure use some more light in here."

I spotted two dented oil lanterns on a shelf behind Henry's workbench. After lighting them, I gave one to Rob, who held it above Andy and frail Uncle Henry. The light glowed down on the old man who was still awake, his eyes glistening. Andy talked to him constantly in a low, calm voice.

When the medics arrived, everyone was shooed from the barn. Andy, Rob and I stood outside under the floodlights illuminating the yard, for what seemed like hours before Henry, a white bandage around his middle and an IV swinging from the post attached to the stretcher, was rolled out and into the ambulance. Andy trotted back to where Jeb was contained.

No sooner had they settled Uncle into the ambulance when Auntie ran from the house, her purse clutched tightly in both hands. "I'm going with him to the hospital," she announced, heading for the big white van. A police car rolled into the yard with lights flashing. She poked her head out before they closed the double doors. "Luther will stay here and help you answer the police's questions."

Rob and I watched the medic examine Jeb, and then jog back to the ambulance. The vehicle, lights blazing and sirens wailing, headed back down the driveway. Next to the barn opening stood the gunman, with his white-gauze bandaged head. Only his mud-streaked face peeked out, his expression grim. Andy nudged Jeb forward, holding the rope binding his hands behind his back like a person would hold a leashed dog, while Officer Cook and another policeman climbed from the car and strode over to them. The uniformed man took over the rope in Andy's hand and escorted Jeb to the patrol car while Officer Cook flipped open a notepad and scribbled something. He smiled when he looked up and spotted Rob and me.

Andy rejoined us while I told Thatcher Cook all that had happened, leaving Whitehead's name out of it along with the part about the screeching and ghostly sounds. I knew if I mentioned anything about that, they wouldn't believe me about the rest. After he'd written down all the details, Officer Cook nodded his head and closed his notepad. Then he carefully placed the knife Uncle had used, Jeb's flashlight and gun in separate plastic bags.

He pointed towards the barn. "What is up there in those rafters anyway?"

I glanced at Andy and shrugged. "I don't really know. Uncle Henry used to own this farm, so he undoubtedly stored old farm equipment or other stuff up there; probably nothing important. Thank you for coming so quickly, Officer Cook."

"We've got him this time, Lorie, and I intend to keep him!" He pulled a flashlight from his belt. "But first, I want to check out the barn, if you don't mind."

"I'll show you," I offered, intending to follow him anyway.

Andy and I went back to the barn with Officer Cook. I noticed Rob watching us out of the corner of my eye.

Andy paused before we reached the barn. "Listen, Lorie. I've got to run back to the house for a minute."

I nodded as he trotted away. Inside the barn, Officer Cook scanned the area with his light and then made a few more notes in his book before bidding me goodbye. I stood inside the barn near the doorway and watched him briefly speak to Rob before climbing into the driver's seat of the patrol car.

Burlus, Luther, Lizzy, and Leroy strolled back towards the house, chattering to each other as they walked. With the crowd gone, everything seemed almost too quiet. When Rob headed back towards the barn, I stepped from view behind a straw bale. As he entered, he called out to me, but I held my breath and remained silent. He stood for a moment before stepping over to where two of the remaining rope knots lay against the post. He ran his fingers over them lightly, peering up. My eyes focused on the frayed rope just under one of those knots. It had nearly been cut before Jeb had come into the barn. Somehow during the fracas that ensued, the rope was severed, with the small length drooped down onto the post. The new rope was taut, holding the mysterious load by itself. The post creaked and groaned from the load it now supported.

As Rob studied the frayed rope, I couldn't stifle a sneeze. He jerked his hand back and spun around. "Lorie?"

"Oh hi." I nonchalantly stepped out from behind the bale, brushing a few strands of straw from my blouse. "I thought I heard one of the cows having a problem back there so I went to check. I didn't realize you'd come in."

He looked back up into the dim ceiling. "Just curious about what could be up there. But I suppose we should check it out tomorrow when we have daylight."

"Good idea," I agreed, glancing at my watch. "Why, it's nearly 10:30. I don't know about you, but I'm exhausted."

"I am as well," conceded Rob. "We'll tackle this bright and early tomorrow, perhaps even before that Easter Bunny hides his eggs."

****

As the weatherman had predicted, a storm blew in that evening. Rain rattled against the windows accompanied by intermittent lightning and thunder, waking me minutes after I'd dozed off. A tree limb banged against the side of the house, startling me awake more than once. By 2:00, the storm had died down and I stumbled out of bed and across the room. I raised the window, breathing in the sweet after-rain air. Back in the warm bed, I pulled the blanket tight around my neck and fell into a deep sleep.

Out of nowhere, a gust of wind burst into my room followed by a loud crash. I bolted upright, eyes wide open. The glow-in-the-dark face on the travel alarm read 4:00. Jumping out of bed, I dashed to the window just in time to see the hazy outline of a man in pants and a sleeveless undershirt run towards the barn. By the time he reached the closed door, three more figures had joined him, appearing magically out of the shadows. They all pulled at the barn door, which seemed to be stuck shut.

I struggled into my jeans, old faded sweatshirt and slid my icy feet into my fuzzy slippers before racing down the stairs. The screen door slammed behind me. As I neared the barn, I recognized Rob, Andy, Burlus and Uncle Luther huddled by the still closed sliding door.

"What happened?" I asked, between huffing and puffing to catch my breath.

Uncle Luther pulled his bathrobe tighter around his rotund belly. "You heard that crash, didn't you? We've been trying to get this door open, but it's either stuck or someone's inside holding it shut."

Just as he said that, Burlus, leaning on the door, jumped away as it creaked and opened a couple of inches. *Maybe simply his weight on it loosened it. Or was it the ghosts? But why are the boys shutting us out?* Andy and Luther pushed it open, shaking their heads as to how easy it had suddenly become.

The moon, dim in the cloudy spring sky, threw very little light into the cavernous room. A large mass loomed at its center in a cloud of dust, particles still floating down from above.

The five of us crept towards the object. Luther, flashlight in his hand, found and lit the pair of hurricane oil lamps hanging just inside the door. He handed Burlus one and held the other as they circled the mysterious object.

"What in the world is it?" asked Rob.

A lumpy rectangular thing with its sides folded up to the middle, so they came to a point, appeared to be tied together with cobwebs. A lengthy, wooden piece stuck out on one side but it seemed to be only partly there. Long sticks poked out at strange angles with bits of translucent fabric hanging on them like skin.

128

After walking around the object several times, Andy and Burlus began severing the ropes binding it.

With each strand that fell away, the object creaked and shuddered, as if it were sighing in relief to finally have the pressure taken off.

"Last rope here," shouted Burlus. "Andy, you and Rob better brace the sides, in case this thing crashes down when I cut it."

When the last rope snapped, the folded-up sides flapped down. The two boys yelled in unison at the falling masses, each catching what appeared to be the wings before they could hit the ground. I noticed a bundle thud to the floor beneath its center, just as Uncle Luther yanked me back under the loft.

While the dust settled, I squinted through the haze. "Why, it looks like a giant bird!" Then I shook my head. "No, I've seen pictures of this in that Gustave Whitehead book. This is one of his planes. I'll bet it's either Number 21 or 22. This might have been the plane he flew back in 1901!"

Rob reached out with his hand to touch what looked like the cockpit seat.

"Stop! Don't touch anything," I shouted. "This could be a valuable part of history. We need to get specialists in here to deal with it before it crumbles."

Rob pulled his hand back. "Yes, of course," he agreed. "Would it be all right if I took some photos of it?"

"I guess so," I said. *Why hasn't he asked the question everyone else has: Who is Gustave Whitehead? He isn't even surprised about finding such an ancient plane. He must know who Whitehead was.* I turned to Andy. "Who do you think we should call about this? Are there any historical societies around here?"

Uncle Luther had been leaning against the loft ladder. "You might try starting with the Museum in Bridgeport. They'd know who to contact."

****

This has been some Easter morning! I felt like skipping as I bounced along with the others as we headed to the house. The glow from the sun on the edge of the horizon dimly lit the yard, sparkling off the puddles and wet grass. The clouds moved aside, opening up patches in the blue sky. Birds sang and a rooster screeched his morning wake-up call. I inhaled the welcome aroma of coffee as it drifted out through the kitchen's screen door. Lizzy, in her full-length red apron, scurried past the window as she fixed breakfast.

"My, you all are up early!" Her high pitched declaration made me smile. "Don't tell me you're out looking for Easter eggs."

Uncle Luther laughed as he led the small group through the kitchen. "We had a delivery, all right," he said, "but I don't think it was from the Easter bunny. There was a little surprise from the barn rafters this morning. Uncle Henry must have stowed that old Whitehead plane up there years and years ago. We'll have to ask him about it when we go see him at the hospital."

Lizzy giggled. "Oh, I nearly forgot! Auntie spoke to the doctor and he said Uncle Henry came through the surgery just fine! They got the bullet out and he'll be able to come home real soon!"

The bacon and eggs and toast and coffee really hit the spot. *Thank goodness Uncle Henry will be all right! I wonder what that mysterious clump was that fell under the plane.* I'm afraid I was overly excited and ended up chattering too much relating what Uncle Henry had said

130

about helping Gustave Whitehead with his planes and flying, back at the turn of the century. Luther questioned me repeatedly, shaking his head in amazement that he'd never heard anything from Uncle Henry about any flying machines or anything else concerning Whitehead. However, when I noticed Rob's empty chair at the table, I stopped in midsentence.

Gulping the last of my orange juice, I stood abruptly and excused myself. I gathered up my plate and glass, slid them into the sink. "I really must get back out to the barn to check on the plane."

No sooner had the screen-door slammed behind me when Rob came out of the barn, an expensive looking camera hanging from his neck. He sure was in a hurry to get pictures of that plane.

Rob waved at me. "Hey, Lorie. I just snapped a few pictures of the plane. Hope they come out OK. Pretty hard to get good pictures with such bad light. I hope there's some hot coffee left."

I winked and nodded. "You'd better get in there or it'll be all gone."

I walked past him towards the barn. Once inside, I closed the door, standing for a moment while my eyes adjusted to the dimness. The lanterns had both been extinguished and the sun through the grubby windows provided weak light.

I stepped around the plane, stopping behind the right wing, where there was a small opening in the boat-shaped body, which might have been the cockpit. Flat on my stomach, I slithered beneath the main body towards the brown, dusty lump situated nearly over the back pair of large bicycle wheels that must have been landing gear. I slid what appeared to be an old leather briefcase out from under the plane. Holding the frail case with both hands, I carried it to Uncle Henry's workbench and placed it on the floor beside several paint cans and underneath a small pile of drop-cloths. Later, when I have more time, I'll come back and examine it. As I stood and brushed the grime from my slacks and blouse, voices drifted in from outside.

I quickly slid through the narrow door opening, almost running into Lizzy, decked out in her pastel pink Easter dress and carrying a pale-green, basket purse.

"Lorie, what are you doing out here?" she asked. "Aren't you coming with us to church?"

"Of course," I replied. "I was just looking for an earring that I thought I might have lost out here earlier. Didn't find it, though. My, you look Eastery in your spring dress."

Lizzy grinned, raising her eyebrows as she eyed my dusty clothes.

"It'll only take me a minute to change," I said, trotting towards the house. "I'll meet you all in the car."

****

It had been ages since I had set foot in a church. Decked out in my new lime-green dress and pearl choker, I tried hard not to trip in my high heels. Although the welcome at the door had been warm, it still felt strange to be the only white person in this colored gathering. Everyone knew Auntie and Uncle Luther, and although people were polite to me, there were uncomfortable stares from most of the congregation. The singing was boisterous and toe-tapping, but with no hymnals; I had trouble joining in. The preacher's rich, baritone filled the tiny church during the sermon and from time to time he slammed his bible down on the podium to emphasize a point (and I was sure it also served to keep people awake). Shouts of "Hallelujah!" and "Praise the Lord" and "Amen" punctured the air like bursts from a busy woodpecker. I squirmed in the slippery pew as beads of sweat trickled down my back. Folks around me fanned themselves with their programs as the minutes crept by. *It's only for an hour and then we can go to the hospital to see Uncle Henry.* With the final prayer and a rousting "Amen!" the preacher strode down the aisle to the front door to greet everyone as they left. I was glad we'd been sitting at the back and therefore were among the first to leave.

****

Uncle Henry was never aware that we had visited that day. According to the nurses, he had awakened earlier, but had gone right back to sleep after breakfast. He was out of intensive care now and in a room with one other colored man and an empty bed. A large white-haired negro nurse greeted our group of relatives and told us that Uncle Henry had come through the surgery fine and might be able to go home in a couple of days. Two other white nurses came in while we were there and walked past us, checked the machines, then left with not even a "hello."

The older of those two nurses clucked her tongue at me, and whispered loudly, "What are you doing here?" My silence was greeted with a dirty look from the other white nurse, so I simply turned my back and ignored them. As much as I wanted to quiz Uncle Henry about the plane in the barn, I doubted I'd even be allowed to visit him if I came alone. I stared down at his prone body; tubes attached to him and the machines rhythmically beeping and humming. *He looks so helpless and old as he lies there.*

A hand grasped my arm from behind, startling me. Rob indicated with a nod that it was time to leave. We left the room, following the rest of the silent relatives.

133

At the top of the front steps of the hospital, Auntie said, "I brought some flowers to put on Mama's grave site, so we'll swing by Lakeview Cemetery. It shouldn't take long."

As I piled into Rob's car with Andy and Lizzy, I said, to no one in particular, "I wonder if Gustave Whitehead is buried at that cemetery?"

"I suppose he is," said Lizzy, "but he'd be in the section with the German immigrants. That won't be anywhere near where Auntie's mama is buried because the colored people have their own spot there. We'll ask Uncle Luther when we stop. He'll know."

The cemetery was brilliant shades of green this time of year. Blossoms filled the trees and a slight breeze brought the salty scent of the ocean. Auntie's mother's grave was set off separate from the rest of the tombstones in a grassy area at the far corner of the cemetery, situated beneath a large, lone oak tree. The plain stones around her grave were identical except for the names and dates. Small, white and chipped around the edges, they almost all had the name "Jackson" on them. A large grassy strip lay between them and the next family named "Lincoln."

Uncle Luther motioned for all of us to stand back away from the stone as Auntie, on her hands and knees placed the flowers gently on the grave and spoke as if her mother were still alive. I whispered in Uncle Luther's ear my request for the location of Whitehead's grave site as he stood and watched Auntie. He coughed into his white handkerchief then pointed towards the south corner of the cemetery.

It was a pleasant walk for Andy, Rob and me, to Gustave Whitehead's grave site. I gasped at the large monument memorialized where he had been buried 40 years before in an unmarked grave. According to the inscription, he had died October 12, 1927 and was buried in a pauper's grave, known thereafter only to cemetery officials as "No. 42." Three years earlier, on August 15, 1964, the State of

Connecticut had honored him with the new monument and proclaimed him the Father of Aviation in Connecticut by Governor John Dempsey, commemorating his flight of August 14, 1901. I read a copy of the Proclamation placed on the monument saying in part, "The Connecticut Aeronautical Historical Association is bringing highly deserved recognition to a pioneer in the field of aviation who has been wholly forgotten by the public, even in the State of Connecticut where his highly important work was carried out." It went on to say that, "In further recognition of Connecticut's forgotten genius, I am pleased to designate August 15th as GUSTAVE WHITEHEAD DAY, and to urge that all honor be accorded to him as The Father of Aviation in Connecticut."

Tears blurred my eyes as I shook my head in amazement. *This is incredible! How could this man, so revered, be so forgotten? Certainly someone connected with the memorial will be delighted with the plane sitting in the barn.* I turned to Uncle Luther, who had just walked up and was reading the plaque. "We must get down to that Bridgeport Museum first thing tomorrow morning."

Uncle Luther shook his head. "This is amazing news. Why, I never knew Uncle Henry was involved with this man and his inventions." He rubbed his jaw and hesitated. "But I'm afraid you'll have to go without me. I have a dental appointment tomorrow and Louise will want to spend more time with Henry. Maybe one of the boys can go with you."

"Sure, Lorie," said Andy. "I'll go with you. I can't believe this was here all along and I didn't know about it. But I'll bet we'll get a ton of information from that museum. Remember, though, we've got to get all this straightened out and get on back to school this week."

"Yes, I'd planned on leaving by Wednesday," I answered, still staring at the stone monument.

"I'll come with you too, Lorie," Rob offered. "I'd like to learn more about this Whitehead fellow."

I thanked them both. *Is he really curious about Whitehead or more interested in what I am going to do with the information? With Jeb in custody, Rob should be out of here and on his way back to Washington.*

****

When we drove into the yard just before noon, the first thing I noticed was that the barn door was wide open. *I distinctly remembered closing it before we left.* As soon as the car stopped, I jumped out and ran into the barn.

Chapter Fifteen

The Forces That Be

The plane was there, all right, in a heap. Propped up in the center of the pile, scrawled in red paint on a slab of wood, was a sign: "Free Firewood." Bamboo poles stuck out at odd angles and bits of fabric and sawdust floated in the air. Struts were smashed or chopped in half. Scattered everywhere, the once bird-shaped wings, ripped and torn into tiny scraps littered the area. The plane was nothing more than a jumbled pile of kindling. An axe leaned on the post like an innocent bystander.

I blinked and looked at the mess, my eyes refusing to focus through the tears. *Who could have done such a thing? And why? Jeb is in jail. Or at least he's supposed to be.*

Tears streamed down my face as I turned and ran for the barn door, almost colliding with Rob, Andy and Lizzy. I pushed past them and kept running, ignoring Rob's shouts. The other car with Uncle Henry, Burlus, Auntie, Leroy and Crystal had parked and was emptying out as I dashed past. I could feel everyone staring at me as the kitchen screen door slammed in my wake.

The phone ringing brought me to a halt. I answered it, recognizing Officer Cook's voice as Andy and Rob burst into the kitchen behind me. I couldn't control the tremble in my voice as he told me the latest news. "He what? But how could you just let him go?" Perched on the stool beside the counter, I stared out the window with the phone receiver held tightly to my ear and my right index finger winding in and out of the coiled cord. "No, I can't prove he did it, but who else would? He broke in and destroyed personal property. I want him arrested and thrown in jail for good this time. I'll sue him for harassment if the other charges are ignored. He won't leave me alone. I'm sure the handwriting on the sign he left can be connected to him. And there must be finger-prints on the axe." I paused and listened for a moment. "Of course I realize it's Easter morning." I blew out my breath loudly. "All right. We'll expect you in 20 minutes." I slammed the phone back onto the receiver.

"They let him go, didn't they?" said Rob.

I nodded, trying to brush away the dampness on my cheeks with my hand. He walked up to me and put his arms around me. I collapsed into his arms and sobbed.

****

From the kitchen window, I watched Officer Cook's car skid to a stop in a cloud of dust from the gravel driveway. The driver's door shot open and out stepped Thatcher, wearing a rumpled gray suit and skinny black tie. He looked like he'd just come from church. The same man who was with him earlier emerged from the passenger's side, this time lugging a large camera.

When I entered the barn, the other policeman was circling the pile, snapping photographs. It was hard to see what he looked like because of the low light in the room, punctuated by the camera's flash popping in rapid succession. Shorter, lighter and younger than Cook, his tangle of black curls bobbed up and down as he clicked pictures every few feet, circling the plane remnants.

Cook knelt beside the axe that still leaned against the smashed plane, scraping something off the floor with a jackknife and putting it into a small glass jar.

My shoes clacked on the plank floor as I stepped closer. Cook looked up, meeting my gaze. "Blood," he said, pointing at several brown blobs on the ground. Bits of straw had been carefully moved aside to uncover a trail of spots leading from one end of the plane to the other, where the axe still rested.

"Whose blood is it?" I whispered.

"That is what I hope to find out," replied Cook, returning to his scraping. "Either someone was with this mad axe man, or he injured himself while destroying this...this whatever it was." He pointed at the stains. "This trail of blood leads towards the door, so watch where you step. In fact, get everyone away from the area and out of the barn now."

As I asked the onlookers to leave, Rob, his camera dangling from around his neck, stepped into the barn, stopping at the doorway. "If it would be of any help, Officer, I took some pictures of the plane earlier, before it was wrecked. The film is still in the camera, but I'll remove it for you. You're welcome to borrow it." He walked behind piled bales and turned his back to us as he fiddled with the camera.

"It would indeed help since I can't imagine what this pile of wood was, let alone how it got here in the first place," said Cook. He rose from his squatting position and clutching his lower back, walked a few steps, stretching as he went.

"It was an old plane, probably one of Gustave Whitehead's from the early 1900's that had been stored in the rafters of this barn and when the ropes were severed, it came crashing down," explained Rob. "I was surprised it remained intact after having fallen."

Cook nodded and turned back to me. "Young lady, that man, Jeb Bracken, whom we arrested earlier, claimed the gun that shot Henry Jackson did not belong to him. He said that when he entered the barn to ask for directions,

Jackson pulled the gun on him and threatened to shoot him. Then when he didn't leave right away, Jackson attacked him and he simply defended himself. Figured the gun must have gone off accidently. He was held overnight for trespassing."

"But that's a lie," I blurted, glaring at Rob as he lightly touched my arm.

"Now take a deep breath before you say any more," he whispered in my ear.

I hate to admit that he's right. I have to calm down and think before saying too much.

"I was in the barn helping Uncle Henry when Jeb came in," I told Cook. "I don't think he actually saw me because I was standing behind a stack of bales. He's the one who pulled the gun on Uncle Henry. And he never once asked for any directions." I shook my head in disbelief. "But I already signed a statement to that effect. Why do you believe him and not me? Besides, his prints must be all over that gun."

"I believe you, Lorie," said Officer Cook with a heavy sigh. "Unfortunately, the prints were so smeared on the gun, they were unidentifiable and Jeb Bracken seems to have some pretty heavy connections in the Department. I don't know how far the man can go before we'll be able to lock him up for good."

"But he almost killed Uncle Henry!" I replied.

"They're calling it an accident. Look on the bright side," began Cook. I glowered at him as he continued. "If this blood is indeed his, he's hurt and not likely to come back right away and if the accident was as bad as this blood indicates, he will have gone to someone for help. We will be checking the local doctors and the hospital to see if anyone with a knife wound has been seen. I'm just sorry we can't fix what he destroyed here."

Officer Cook assured Auntie, Uncle Luther and me that he would be in contact with them as soon as he had any information concerning Jeb's whereabouts. Rob handed Cook the roll of film with the promise that copies of the prints would be sent to him. Although I was uneasy about the safety of the film, there was nothing I could do except wait until it was developed.

****

Easter dinner was quite the repast. The sparkling dinnerware winked at me when I entered the dining room. Tiny pink roses with dark green leaves and stems delicately bordering the cream-colored background on the plates, reminded me of Grandmother's china that was only used for holiday dinners. The sterling silverware, skirting the edges of the plates, gleamed in the sunlight blazing in the side windows. I felt a lump in my throat remembering the holiday dinners from years past, but swallowed hard and took a deep breath before pulling out the chair at my place at the corner. *That was then and this is now.*

Steaming platters of ham and turkey at the far end of the table filled the room with mouth-watering smells. A huge salad bowl dominated the other end. In between, were scattered bowls of peas and pearl onions, glazed carrots, and mashed potatoes. An intricately carved silver ladle poked its handle out of the brimming gravy tureen and a basket of linen-covered rolls sat by my plate. At each place was an individual green gelatin salad in the shape of a bunny. Uncle Henry's vacant chair made me sad. His place had been set as though he was expected to appear at any moment, but I knew better. *At least he's still hanging in there.*

The supper prayer was somber and brief. Spoons clanked and scraped as plates were heaped with food. Even though everyone raved about the fare, an aura of sadness hovered over us. Andy retraced what had happened to Uncle Henry in the barn while people just shook their heads in disbelief that something so tragic could have happened to someone they knew and loved. Auntie tried to be optimistic with her insistence that Uncle was as tough as they came and would be just fine.

After supper, the boys found a basketball game on TV while the women did the dishes and took care of the food. *Some things never change.* I dribbled dish soap into the sink piled with dirty plates. But, with all the girls help, it took less than an hour before I untied my apron. Then, I rushed upstairs to change into my sweatshirt, jeans and windbreaker, anxious to get out to the barn and the brief-case, hopefully just where I'd left it. *There has to be more proof than that film Rob handed over.*

****

The barn door slid open just far enough for me to slip in. I tried to breathe quietly as I tiptoed across the wooden planks to the workbench. The stillness seemed tense, like a cat crouched to leap on its prey. I looked around, with the uneasy feeling that someone was watching me.

The briefcase was still there under the drop-cloth. Caked with dust and cobwebs, the leather was brittle and dark from age. My fingerprints, where I had grabbed it from underneath the plane, seemed to be the only marks on it. *Perhaps because it has been stored so far above ground, mice weren't able to gnaw at the case and its contents. It seems intact.*

I lifted it with both hands and carried it to an empty stall at the far side of the barn where I wouldn't be surprised by visitors until I'd seen its contents. Placing the leather case on the straw-strewn ground, I knelt before it, carefully folding the lid back. It cracked at the top as it opened. I

142

winced, thinking it might break off altogether as I tilted it back on the floor. When I reached inside, the dead body of a huge spider fell out, landing on my bent knee. Squealing, I leaped back, clamping both hands over my mouth, hoping no one heard. All remained quiet. With the case tipped up, I peered inside before extracting mechanical drawings, letters, and pages of notes, all scrawled in the same pinched writing. However, the handwriting seemed to be in German, my two years of the language in college were not enough to decipher it.

As I peered back inside the case, a small bundle still lay at the bottom, wrapped in a handkerchief. I grasped it gently with both hands, afraid it might crumble. The string holding it together pulled apart with little effort and the thin handkerchief fell away, revealing a stack of old photos. Even though they'd been protected, they were faded and some stuck together. I gingerly pried them apart, amazed that the pictures had lasted as long as they had in this damp barn.

Each picture featured Whitehead's planes, No. 21 or No. 22, and on the back side were scribbled names and dates in that same tight script. I recognized many of the pictures that looked similar to the ones included in the book by Stella Randolph. However, there were a few I had never seen. In one, a group of children stood in front of the plane, and in another, Whitehead's young daughter, Rose sat beside No. 21. But it was the last picture that caught my attention. In it, a plane hovered about ten feet over the ground. The mustached pilot, visible as he peered down from the cockpit, looked like the pictures of Whitehead. I flipped the picture over and saw the words "G. Whitehead" scrawled across its back with the date "16 August, 1901" beneath. *Oh my God!*

The barn door creaked. I slipped the picture into my jacket pocket and hurriedly wrapped the remaining photos back in the handkerchief. Deep into the leather case they went, followed by the stack of papers. The crisp leather top cracked further as I folded it closed. With both hands, I

143

grasped the case and stood up, just as Rob stepped around into the stall.

"Here you are. I wondered where you'd gone," he said. His eyes focused on the bundle in my arms. "What have you got there?"

"Oh, I found this old case right after the plane fell. It must have fallen from the cockpit. I dragged it to safety before we left the barn this morning and it's a good thing I did. Otherwise it might have been destroyed along with the plane," I said.

His steady gaze never blinked as he half-smiled. "Really. Well, let's go out on the workbench and have a look." He followed me out of the stall.

It didn't take long to spread all of the papers and pictures out on the bench. Rob looked at each one carefully before setting it down, saying nothing until they were all displayed.

"It looks like the original plans and pictures all right. Unfortunately, these photos are so old that they are beginning to fade," he exclaimed, holding one up to the light. Then he asked, "Were you able to contact anyone at the Museum in Bridgeport yet?"

"I tried to call there earlier, but nobody answered. It is probably closed, being Easter and all. Maybe I can reach someone tomorrow. I sure hope so because I'm leaving to go back to school on Tuesday morning."

Although I hadn't remembered it being windy outside, the closed barn door clattered almost as if someone had hit it. Straw sprinkled down from the loft and the whole building creaked and groaned. I thought I heard children whimpering up above. "Did you hear that?" I whispered to Rob, as I looked up at the rafters.

"Hear what?" He craned his neck as he too peered up through the gloom. "Probably just mice."

We both stood still and listened as more bits of straw trickled down, landing on the papers covering the work-bench.

Rob took two steps back and cleared his throat. "While we have all these plans and pictures out, I think I'll run in and get my camera and take a few pictures before anything happens to them."

Chapter Sixteen

Protection

There is something about Rob that doesn't feel right. I'm so giddy and breathless around him, especially when he touches me. But why is he still hanging around here? He said he was keeping an eye on Jeb, yet Jeb was arrested and he doesn't really seem to care. Is there some other reason he has remained here? Could it have something to do with Whitehead? He seems awfully eager to photograph the plane and the contents of the case. I paced in front of the workbench while Rob retrieved his camera, my hand cradling the picture in my pocket. *I won't tell him about that photo. Not yet, anyway. It would be smarter to put it someplace besides the barn.* I headed for the open door. Before I could even touch it, the door slammed shut. *Oh no, not again!*

I drew out the photo and stared at it. *Maybe, just maybe...* I ran back to the stall where I had examined the briefcase contents. An old rusty plow sat in the far corner. Grabbing its handles, I tried to move it but it seemed welded to the floor. Over and over again, I lunged against it but it still wouldn't budge. Dropping to my knees, I cringed at the spider webs woven between the blades as I felt around the pitted metal. There was just enough space to poke the photo between them, so I slid it in until it disappeared. Coming to my feet, I wiped my dirty hands on my jeans and stared down at the spot where I'd put the picture. Nothing showed. *That will do for now.*

The barn door creaked open. *Rob is back.* I stepped around the corner of the stall and slipped into the large main room.

"Hey, why did you close the door?" Rob said. "You knew I was coming back."

146

"I didn't want the papers to blow off the bench," I said, out of breath. When he glanced back from where I'd been, I hastily added, "I was just making sure I hadn't dropped anything from the briefcase."

Rob, with his camera on a strap around his neck and a tripod in hand, sauntered over to the laid out collection. "It's so dark in here; I'm going to have to use the flash." He extended the tripod's legs and clamped them into place, then added, "In order to get sharp, clear pictures, I need this."

I walked over to the open door and stepped out into the sunlight while he set up the camera. *Hmmm. Now I can leave the barn, since I don't have the picture with me. I can't believe it. We should be able to leave with the other photos and papers.*

Once he got all set up, it didn't take long to photograph the documents. He did them as a group and individually. He sure is comfortable with that camera.

With the final click of the shutter, Rob unscrewed the camera from the tripod, folded the leather case around it and snapped it shut. He motioned towards the documents. "I think we should just carry them carefully into the house, just in the case." He handed me a loose pile, his fingers lingering underneath them as he laid them in my hands and looked into my eyes. "Here, can you take this stack of drawings?" Then he reached over my out-stretched arms and brushed my lips with a kiss.

For a moment, I forgot how to breathe, then inhaled sharply and cleared my throat. Still, my voice was barely above a whisper. "We'd better get these inside."

His reply was low and breathless. "I'll bring that bundle of photos." With the camera strap slung over his shoulder, he gathered up the tripod in one hand and the pictures in the other. Side by side, we walked back to the house.

The late afternoon sun was still bright, even though it hung low in the sky. The long shadow from the barn reminded me of stories from my childhood about giants roaming the earth and the great shadows they cast. Rob's arm brushed my side as we walked, sending a chill through me. It could have been due to the cool breeze that tugged at my hair, but I didn't really believe that.

Once in the house, Andy, Burlus, and Auntie crowded in around Rob and me as we spread the documents out on a card table in the living room. Andy, studying the photographs, shook his head. "These are all nice, but there's no proof of his flights here. We should take these to the hospital and let Uncle see them. Maybe they would jog his memory."

"These papers should be moved as little as possible to preserve them. He can see them when he returns home," said Rob.

Andy shrugged as I pulled him aside. "Let's go out to the barn for a minute. I need to talk to you."

"Why? What's wrong?"

I shushed him while motioning him to come along.

He raised an eyebrow but followed. I noticed Rob watching as we left, but he didn't follow us. *I'll have to keep an eye out for him.*

Andy closed the barn door at my insistence. "Now what's going on? Why all the secrecy?"

"There is something I want to show you." I scanned the room before leading him into the stall with the plow. On hands and knees beside the rusty relic, I poked and prodded my fingers under the blade that rested on the ground, finally extracting the dusty photo.

148

Andy wiped the straw and smudges from it, turning it over to read the back as well. "Holy Moley! Why isn't this one in there with the others? This is it! This is the proof!"

"Yeah, I know." I looked Andy in the eye. "I was afraid something would happen to it, like what happened to the plane. I want to protect it. You're the only one I trust to know about it. If we keep it to ourselves, maybe we can keep it safe."

"But wouldn't it be safer in the house?" he asked.

"Well, I would have taken it in, except...I couldn't get it out of the barn," I whispered. "I put it in my pocket and tried to leave, but the door mysteriously shut and I could not get it open. I think the boys' ghosts don't want it to leave here."

He threw up his hands and shook his head. "Oh, now, that's just plain crazy. Don't tell me you believe what Uncle told you about this barn being haunted." Then he slid the photo in his pants pocket and returned to the workbench area. "I'll carry it out if you're afraid."

I followed him, a smile tugging at the corners of my mouth. I stopped a few feet from the door and folded my arms across my chest as Andy grabbed the door latch. He heaved and grunted before sliding to the ground when the door wouldn't budge. Standing up, he brushed off his pants and grabbed it firmer. It still wouldn't move.

"This is ridiculous," he said through clenched teeth, yanking at it again and again.

"Here," I held out my hand. "Give me the picture then try to open it." He laid it in my palm, his unblinking eyes big and round. This time, the door slid open with no trouble. Andy tiptoed forward, peeking out around it on both sides. No one was out there.

149

"See, it must just have been stuck. All that pulling I did probably loosened it up," he insisted, standing up straight.

"Right." I took one step towards the open door but it slid shut in front of me. I jumped back, stumbling to the ground, the picture still in my hand.

Andy's voice cracked, "Are you OK? Lorie, answer me!"

I took a deep breath. "I'm fine. Listen, I'm going to put the picture back where it was. It's better if we just leave it here for now. Wait for me, would you?"

"Sure thing."

This is ridiculous! I shook my head and walked back to the stall. After sliding the picture back under the plow, I peered down at it from all angles, making sure it couldn't be seen. I had a gut feeling that I shouldn't leave it there. *But then, if I can't get it out, then no one else can. Whatever force keeps it in can be trusted to keep it safe.*

I slid open the barn door and walked back to the house with Andy. "Let's just keep this between us, OK?"

He glanced back at the barn. "Don't worry. My lips are sealed."

****

That night I fell into bed, exhausted from the day's events. Tossing and turning, I dreamed of climbing a steep rock wall when panicked voices shouting, "Fire! Fire!" interrupted. I bolted upright, my arms covered with goose-bumps. The clock glowed 3:30. The stench of burning wood, along with indistinct voices drifted through the open

150

window. A fire siren in the distance grew louder by the second as I raced to the window and yanked back the curtain.

The floodlight illuminated two figures rushing towards the barn, carrying buckets and garden hoses. Flames licked through the side window up the north face of the barn on the driveway side. I was sure one of the people was Rob and the other, Andy. Soon, streams of hose water disappeared into the spreading blaze.

With flashing red lights and sirens whining down, a bright red firetruck skidded to a halt by the barn door. Seven or eight men leapt out and extracted giant hoses. In minutes, fountains of water smothered the fire, leaving nothing but a cloud of smoke.

"Oh no!" I said out loud as I watched. "The picture! I've got to get to it before it's ruined!"

I threw on my dirty jeans and sweatshirt, then dashed down the stairs and out to the barn. Pungent smoke stung my eyes as I squinted at the burned out area. Uncle Luther came coughing through the haze, leading a cow and two wild-eyed horses through the open door. Before I could enter, a hand grabbed my shoulder, bringing me to a stop.

"You can't go in there yet. It's not safe," said a grey-haired fireman, his hat in his other hand.

"But you don't understand..." I began.

"No, you don't understand." He tightened the grip on my shoulder. "If you go in there and get hurt, it would be my hide hanging out to dry. My Captain would come down on me heavy for letting you through."

Andy walked slowly out of the barn, his clothes sooty and dripping, his shoes caked with mud and straw. I waved to him. "Andy! You've got to help me. You know what I had to leave in there," I said. His bewildered expression made me grimace and nod excitedly towards the barn. "The plow. Is the plow OK?" I shouted.

His eyes widened. "Oh, my gosh! I forgot all about that! I'll go back in and see. You stay here," Andy said, trotting towards the door.

"Whoa there," said another fireman.

Andy stopped and turned. "But I need to just run in and check something out," he insisted. "It won't take a minute."

"Nope," said the second fireman, removing his hat. Underneath, a mop of curly blond hair sprang out in all directions in stark contrast to his blackened face. "No one goes back in there until the inspector gets here and collects any evidence. We think there may have been more than one person responsible for that fire."

Chapter Seventeen

Fred

I looked over at Andy. "More than one man?"

Andy glanced at the fireman, who nodded in confirmation before turning to me. "There's evidence that a man was inside and broke through the window getting out."

I couldn't believe my ears! "You don't suppose it was Jeb Bracken again! I thought he'd be miles from here by now. He already destroyed the plane and almost killed Uncle Henry. Why in the world would he come back to destroy the barn?"

Rob, damp and covered in soot, walked up beside me. "Oh, it was Jeb all right, but he had help."

"What? How do you know?"

"When I woke up to the sound of glass breaking outside in the yard earlier, and went to the window, I saw a man set down a gasoline can and light a handful of what looked like rags. Then he threw it in the broken window there at the side." He pointed at the charred opening by the door.

"But how do you know he wasn't Jeb?" I challenged.

"This man was old, white-haired and stooped. I was inside the house right after he yelled and threw in the rags. The man dropped his gas can and limped off at a trot down the driveway. Through the barn window I could see the flames. Then Bracken came crashing through the broken glass head first and took off after him." Rob wiped his mouth with his sleeve before continuing. "By the time I got downstairs and to the barn, the fire had spread. Andy was already there with the hose and some buckets so I stayed and helped him rather than chasing those two."

"But how did you know it was Jeb?" insisted Lorie.

"Before he dashed from the barn, he stopped for a moment and with the light from the flames, I saw his face. It was him, all right. I'd know him anywhere," Rob said with certainty. "After all, he's why I'm here."

"I wonder what Jeb expected to find here?" I said out loud. *He doesn't know about the picture.*

Rob shook his head. "I can't imagine, but I intend to find out."

****

By Monday morning at 7:00, the smoke had cleared and the trucks and police vehicles had left. The burned out stench still hung in the air as I crept into the barn. In the blackened stall, the old metal plow was all that remained. Most of the wooden plank floor under it had been burned away leaving the plow sitting at an angle, half-in and half-out of the broken floor. I knelt beside it and reached underneath where the picture had been jammed. My fingers felt for the photo, finding nothing but dirt and soot. *It just isn't there; probably destroyed by either the fire or the water used to put it out.*

I stared at the pitiful plow. *Why? Why?* Tears ran down my cheeks and I savagely wiped them away with my arm.

A small voice from behind startled me. "Fred Hawkston started the fire."

I stood and looked around. *Nobody is there.* "What?"

154

"Fred Hawkston started the fire. We saw him," said the voice again.

I scanned the whole area, and then crept out into the main barn, pausing at the workbench, which had escaped the flames. "Where are you? Who are you?"

Two young boys appeared standing side by side in front of the closed barn door. I squinted through the smoky haze, trying to focus on the shimmering forms. They stood there in dirty overalls. Unruly curly hair hung into their eyes and, in back, touched the collars of their dingy undershirts. I blinked and rubbed my eyes when I saw the barn door through their bodies. The taller one spoke, "We saw old man Hawkston light that fire. We tried to stop him but he ran away."

I tried twice before I could find my voice. "H-How did you know who he was?"

"He's the one who attacked us that night in the barn. We heard Henry tell you about the attack. We told Henry not to tell, but he did. Don't worry. The photograph is safe. Fred Hawkston must pay for what he did to us and our Ma and Pa," said the taller boy.

"You have the picture?" I asked, noticing the barn cat washing its face on the floor behind the figures.

"Hawkston must pay. He must pay..." the boy said as they faded away. The cat sprinted across the floor in front of me.

I shook my head and blinked, but the boys were gone. *That picture has to be here somewhere.* I searched the workbench area. Beneath a rusty gallon of brown paint on the lowest shelf, I noticed a scrap of newspaper. As I picked up the heavy can, the paper stuck to its bottom. Pealing it off carefully, so as not to rip it, I was stunned by the 1912 date in the corner. The headline read: Deputy Hawkston Dis-

155

missed Pending Investigation. *There is that name again! Was he the same man the boys were talking about? It's certainly not a common name. Fred Hawkston? If he's still alive, he'd have to be pretty old by now.* Most of the article had been destroyed by the paint from the can, so I couldn't make out why he was dismissed. But as I headed towards the house, I wondered just how many Hawkstons there were in the Bridgeport/Fairfield phone directory.

****

Just my luck, I mused, hanging up the phone. *The Bridgeport Museum is closed until Thursday because the curator is off on a holiday trip.* I thumbed through the directory until I reached the "H's." *Well, there's only one Hawkston in the book. Here goes nothing.* After dialing the phone, it rang at least six times before a woman's gruff voice answered. "Hello."

"Is Fred Hawkston there?" I asked.

"No, he's out. Who is this?"

I ignored her question. "Do you know when he might be back or where I might reach him?"

"What is this about?"

"This matter concerns the Stromberg farm," I answered, in a business-like tone. "It's important I speak with him."

There was a pause before she retorted, "Those Strombergs been dead a long time. What's Fred have to do with that?"

"It's a police matter," I said. *Well, it was, sort of.* "Now where can I reach him?"

There was such a long silence that I was afraid she might have hung up. "Don't know where he is right now," she finally replied. "He'll probably be at O'Malley's near the park for lunch right at noon. But I wouldn't disturb him there, if I was you."

"Thank you for the..." I started to say, but the line went dead.

I glanced at the clock above the kitchen sink. 8:30. I sighed, glancing at the wall calendar. *It's already Monday. Well, I'll have to try to talk to him today because I must be on the road by Wednesday to make it home in time for work Friday.*

Andy burst into the kitchen and yanked open the refrigerator door. Lizzie slipped by, pushing him away as she reached in front grabbing the eggs and bacon. "You two just sit on over there and I'll fix the breakfast."

Andy grinned and slid out the chair opposite me at the kitchen table.

As we ate, I told him quietly, so Lizzie wouldn't hear, about the visit with the boys in the barn and my calls to the Museum along with the attempt to find Fred Hawkston. He'd never heard of any Fred Hawkston.

I stood, snatching up my plate and announced I was going in to town to talk to him and asked Andy if he'd come along. He laid down his fork with an abrupt clank. "Are you sure you want me to go with you. You really shouldn't go alone but you know how people react when they see the two of us together. Maybe you should go with Rob instead. Folks might be more willing to talk to you without a colored boy hanging around." He looked out the window, then back at me. "By the way, where is Rob?"

157

"I haven't seen him this morning yet." I also glanced out the window at the driveway. "But his car is gone, so maybe he went to hunt for Jeb."

"Well, we could wait a while for him," suggested Andy.

"I'd rather you come with me anyway. I don't care what anyone thinks when they see us together." I gave my plate to Lizzie. "Thanks for the wonderful breakfast."

I hurried upstairs to get my purse. *Andy's right. I sure wish Rob had hung around to go with me. But Rob seemed pretty angry about Jeb yesterday, so that must be why he took off so early this morning. I'll just have to hope Andy can control his temper.*

****

Since we didn't need to be at O'Malley's until lunchtime, I suggested we stop by the hospital to visit Uncle Henry and ask him what he knew about Hawkston.

This time when they walked into his room, Uncle Henry was sitting up and in full voice. "What do you call this slop? It can't be food and I'm not about to eat something I don't recognize," he bellowed, motioning towards the tray before him. "Get this what-ever-it-is out of my sight. Now!"

Andy looked back at me and grinned, then turned to Henry. "I see you're feeling better, Uncle."

"Well, I'd be a whole lot better if I could get something decent to eat," he sputtered. When he saw me step out from behind Andy, his eyes softened. "What are you two doing here anyway?"

I nodded towards the nurse who was adjusting the IV bottles and various machines that beeped and whirred around them. Henry prodded the nurse with the edge of his call button devise. "Hey, can't you see I have visitors?"

The colored nurse glanced at Andy and me, pursed her lips, then turned and stomped out, firmly pulling the door shut behind her.

Andy and I scooted two chairs next to Uncle Henry's bed while I told him of the fallen plane that was destroyed, the Whitehead picture I'd hidden in the barn, the fire and escape of Jeb and finally about the encounter with the boys. I also mentioned that the boys claimed to have seen Fred set the fire. He stared into space as he listened.

"So, does the name Fred Hawkston mean anything to you?" I asked.

"Can't say that it does." Henry stroked his chin in thought. Then he added, "But now that I think about it, I do recall the man who was the ringleader that night was named 'Fred,' but I never knew his last name. I'd probably recognize that face, though. Do you know if he's still around?"

"Yes. Andy and I are going to meet him at a place called 'O'Malley's' near the park in town at noon today. I sure wish you could be there too," I told him.

Henry wagged his finger at us. "You both be careful around that fellow. If he is the same one, that man has the conscience the size of a pea."

I thought for a moment. "Am I right in thinking he didn't see you there that night?" I asked. "You were hiding, right?"

"No, I don't think he saw me then or the next day when he and his cronies came back," said Henry. He added, with a slight smile, "Besides, we all look alike anyway, don't you know."

"So you think you could identify him if you saw him?"

"Real possible. Sure like to try," he said.

Andy leaned closer. "Do you know when they are going to release you?"

Henry nodded. "The doctor said I could go home tomorrow morning. So, you all should pick me up as soon as possible." He glanced down at this food tray and added, "Before I starve to death."

Andy stifled a laugh.

I bit at my lip. "Would it be all right if I can convince Fred Hawkston to come by the barn tomorrow afternoon after you're home?"

Uncle Henry half smiled. "I can't think of anyone I'd rather see."

****

O'Malley's Bar and Grill was directly across from the city park. Since the entire street in front of the place was restricted from parking, Andy pulled his car into a lot by the Courthouse, a block away, and we walked back. The old clock on City Hall's tower bonged 12 times as a stream of people pushed through the old wooden door, with the word "O'Malley's" staggered diagonally in large curly letters, outlined in green shamrocks and small dancing leprechauns.

Inside, the hazy air reeked of cigarette smoke, beer and fried food. As we entered, several people looked our way. Some of them pointed and laughed and others shook

160

their heads. They all moved away as Andy walked by, as if he had some communicable disease. In spite of the crowd, I had an overwhelming sense of sadness and loneliness as I stood there with Andy. The bartender, a tall, bald man with a long, sad face, as he moved along the bar nonstop. People in jeans and business suits filled the stools and most of the tables. From the back of the room came a hardy uproar of laughter.

One bushy-faced, broad man came elbowing through the mass up to the bar and slammed down his empty mug. His cheeks glowed brick-red as he bellowed at the bartender. "Old Juniper just broke the record with three bulls-eyes in a row! That calls for a celebration. He said he'd buy for the whole gang, Bert!"

Andy peered over the sea of heads to the dark gloom of the back room. Someone yelled "Mugs Away!" I stood on tiptoe trying to see what was going on when the glint of a dart caught my attention as it thunked into the target. I nudged Andy. "Ask the bartender about you-know-who."

Andy nodded and edged in between bar stools. Folks moved away so as not to touch him. I shook my head. *Maybe it wasn't such a good idea to ask Andy along instead of waiting for Rob.* Andy shouted at the bartender, "Hey, Bert, can you point out Fred Hawkston for me? I was supposed to meet him here today."

Bert's hands were a blur as he pulled beers, built cocktails, replenished dwindling supplies and cleaned the bar top. If he had even heard Andy, he was ignoring him. "Hey Bert," Andy yelled louder.

A stringy-haired, pudgy brunette perched on the stool by his elbow and nudged his arm. "Honey, he'll never answer you. This is the busiest time of day. If you're looking for Fred, he'd be back there at the dart boards." She pointed to the back of the room where a commotion had just occurred. "Are you sure it's Fred you want? He don't take kindly to colored folks, if you know what I mean."

I pulled Andy away and stood on tiptoe to reach his ear, above the din. "Don't take this wrong, Andy. But maybe I'd better ask the questions. I don't want to cause any trouble."

Before he could answer, I pushed through the crowd to the back. Glancing over my shoulder, I noticed he was only a few heads behind. Then I saw the hat and stopped. I looked back at Andy and nodded, then continued towards the man with the hat. Fly-fishing lures hung helter-skelter from it just as they had the night Andy and I had seen him in the cafe when we'd first arrived.

A waitress in a black, skimpy mini-skirt and dark fishnet stockings fought upstream in the crowd, her tray held high above her head. "Come on, let me through, boys," she shouted, shoving men aside with her free hand.

I yelled as she stepped past. "Hey, which one is Fred?"

The waitress paused and glanced over her shoulder before screaming back, "The one in the crazy fishing hat." Then she pushed on through the crowd, her path disappearing shut behind her.

Fred stood in the center of a group of white-haired men laughing and gesturing with a beer mug in one hand and a fist full of darts in the other. As he thrust his mug into the air to emphasize the punch-line of a joke, it crashed into the head of a man standing nearby. The man sank to his knees, holding his head. Fred looked at his empty mug, then down at him. He said something indistinguishable then threw back his head and burst out with a high pitched cackle. When the man stumbled to his feet, he glared at Fred and gestured obscenely before stomping away. The other men stepped aside silently as he left.

162

I hesitated, unsure if I really wanted to break into that cluster of drinking men. Then a touch on my shoulder made it all clear. I smiled back at Andy standing behind me.

With determination, I boldly stepped through the crowd and approached the old man. "Are you Fred Hawkston?"

He leered at me. The area suddenly became still as everyone watched.

Fred slammed his beer mug onto the wooden table beside him, along with his fist full of darts. "Well, who do we have here?" He extended a bony hand towards my breast.

I jerked out of his reach, feeling my face heat up. I must have inadvertently stepped on someone's foot because I suddenly lost my balance and fell against Andy, who caught me and prevented the fall. I muttered a "thanks" before facing the old man again. "I need to talk to you."

"Well, all I have on me now is..." he reached into his pocket and yanked out a hand full of bills and change, throwing it onto the table. "Let's see here. Looks like 23 dollars and 52 cents. That should be enough for at least a quick lick." He laughed and the others roared with him.

"I came to ask you about the fire last night out at the old Stromberg farm. I have it on good authority that you set it," I blurted.

The room became even deathly silent. Fred's grin transformed into a grimace. Then he gestured towards Andy. "Hey look, boys, she brought her nigger boyfriend along." There were a few chuckles, but mostly people were quiet.

"Well, did you?" demanded Andy.

"Did you hear something?" Fred said, elbowing the bald man standing beside him. "Someone must have farted." There were a few chortles.

I took a step forward. "You know, there was an eye witness."

Fred reached out and clamped down on my shoulder with his bony hand. "You best mind your own business, Missy, or you and your nigger here could end up...injured... in some alley."

Andy leaned over and pushed Fred's hand off my shoulder. "Don't touch her, you worthless piece of shit," he said, staring hard at him.

By now, the men standing around them had stopped talking and laughing. Fred's fists were clutched at his sides as he spat through clenched teeth. "Boy, you keep your filthy black paws off of me. Don't ever touch me again." Then he turned toward me. "Ain't nobody saw nothing. You can't prove nothing."

I took a step back from Fred, forcing Andy to move behind as well. "If you don't believe me, meet us at the old Stromberg farm tomorrow at 2:00. That is, if you're not too afraid. Our witness would love to see you again."

Fred lunged forward but his cronies held him back, telling him to calm down and let it go. I heard him swear as Andy and I turned and wove back through the crowd and out the front door.

We had walked halfway back to the car before either of us spoke. "Do you think he'll show up tomorrow?" asked Andy.

"Oh, he'll be there."

Chapter Eighteen

Murder

The sun lay low in the sky as I glanced out the kitchen window, putting the last rinsed pot in the dish rack. *Rob still hasn't shown up and it's almost time for supper.* "Auntie, shall I set the table yet?" I asked, drying my hands.

"There's no rush, but you go right ahead. I don't expect the stew to be done for another 20 minutes or so."

With both hands full of silverware and fresh linen napkins wedged under my arm, I stepped into the dining room, just as the phone rang.

"It's for you, Lorie," Auntie called from the stove. Dumping the silverware and napkins on the table, I stepped back into the kitchen. Auntie motioned to the receiver on the counter.

"Who is it?" I whispered to Auntie, covering the mouthpiece with one hand.

"It's that nice Officer Cook from Bridgeport. He insists on talking to you."

With a deep sigh, I put the receiver to my ear. "Hello? Officer Cook?"

"Lorie, something strange is going on," he said. "Remember that film Rob handed me of the plane before it was wrecked? Well, the boys at the lab tell me it's totally blank. There were never any pictures on it. Don't you think that's odd? Why would he do that?"

"No pictures on it? That is strange," I said. My thoughts drifted back to that moment in the barn when he circled the wreck, snapping photos.

"Are you there?" boomed Cook's voice.

"Yes, sorry. Rob was always so careful with his pictures. He seemed more like a professional photographer than just a guy with a camera. I wish I could ask him about it, but he's not here right now. And I don't know where he went. But when he gets back, I'll certainly find out."

"The contact number he left with me has been disconnected. When you see him, would you have him call me?"

"Certainly," I said. "Oh, by the way, could you do me a favor?"

I filled Officer Cook in on the Stromberg case from long ago and told him I might have a lead on the man responsible for those deaths. I didn't mention the ghost-boys in the barn or their claim to have seen Hawkston set the fire, but did mention the old article that had clung to the paint can on Uncle Henry's workbench with Hawkston's name. Cook said he'd pull up the files on the case and review it.

"That's not all. Fred Hawkston will be out here to talk with Uncle Henry, Andy and me tomorrow at 1:30 in the barn. Even though he's an elderly man now, I don't trust him. He has a vile temper and may be dangerous. I'd feel better if you could be here, just in case."

"1:30? I'll be there and I'll bring someone with me. But I'm afraid I have to be back here by 2:30 for a meeting. Let's hope your visitor is on time."

****

166

Tuesday after lunch, Andy and I guided Uncle Henry slowly into the dim, dank barn. We left the sliding doors open for extra light and to air it out while showing Uncle Henry the fire damage. Upon seeing the burned out stalls and scorched walls, the old man shook his head. "Why would anyone want to torch this beautiful old barn? Thank goodness the Whitehead papers are safe in the house. I'm so sorry the plane couldn't be saved."

"Uncle Henry, I have to tell you that when the boys spoke to me yesterday about Fred Hawkston, they mentioned that they'd seen him light the fire the other night. That's how I convinced him to come out here," I explained. "But why would he want to torch the barn? What's he afraid we'll find?"

"Good question," replied Henry. "I'm sure he doesn't know me from Adam. Maybe he heard something about us finding the plane. But you haven't talked to anyone about that, have you?"

I shook my head. "No. I called the Museum but they were closed, so I haven't been able to talk to anyone about it." I looked at Andy. "The girls would not have said anything to any of their friends, would they?"

He laughed. "Naw. All them girls talk about are boys and clothes."

"Then, it must have been Jeb that he talked to," I concluded. "After all, Rob said he saw Jeb here that night, too. Perhaps Fred and Jeb got together and were afraid there was more hidden evidence in the plane that Jeb might have missed when he chopped it up, so they decided to just get rid of everything."

"Say, where is Rob?" asked Andy

"You know, I'll bet he went off to find Jeb. After all, that's why he's been hanging around, isn't it?" I'm just surprised he hasn't returned or at least called.

****

After settling Uncle Henry on a stool behind the workbench, surrounded by his paints and another tattered birdhouse, Andy followed me back to the stall with the charred plow. He reached underneath, feeling through the straw and soot, hoping that the picture might have been shoved back. But there was no photo, only black mud. As he stood up, there was a loud creak from above and dust particles drifted through the air from the rafters above. We looked at each other with wide eyes, and then crept back to the workbench.

Officer Cook strolled through the open doors and greeted us. "Good to see you've recovered," he said, shaking Henry's hand. "Hope you don't mind, but I pulled our car around to the back side of the barn, so your visitor won't know we're here."

I nodded. "Good idea. The less he knows the better."

Accompanying Cook was another uniformed policeman who towered above us all and extended his hand towards Uncle Henry. "Monroe here, sir. I heard you were a witness to those Stromberg deaths here back in 1912." His smiling young face was blanketed with a mass of freckles and curly, red hair peeked out from under his police cap. A Billy club swayed from his belt when he moved.

"This young fellow is a history nut," explained Cook. "He's been researching that old case."

"Yes, and what a fascinating one it is. Did you know that Fred Hawkston was a sheriff's deputy that night in

168

1912?" Monroe said. "I came across the records concerning his termination less than a week after the Stromberg deaths. It seems that the department kept the whole thing pretty quiet when they fired him. But there is no indication as to why they kicked him out. Maybe they didn't have any solid evidence to prove his guilt."

I remembered the clipping where I'd seen Hawkston's name. I'd forgotten to mention to Uncle Henry about Fred being a law officer. "Did you know Fred was a deputy?"

"I didn't see any badge, but it wouldn't surprise me," Henry said. "The county sheriff was a known negro-hater back then and hired mostly relatives or friends who thought likewise."

Cook glanced around the room, his gaze resting on the ladder leading to the loft. "How about we watch from up there?"

Andy nodded. "That would be fine place to stay out of sight, but you have to be especially quiet because any movement at all will cause straw to fall and give you away."

Two o'clock came and went and all was still. Uncle Henry sat behind his workbench and repaired the trim on the cracked roof of the birdhouse. Andy leaned against a beam and whittled on an old piece of gnarled oak.

I explored all of the corners of the barn, and then returned to the main room, brushing cobwebs and dirt from my jeans before perching on an old three-legged wooden milking stool leaning against the wall by the workbench. A soft, staccato snore drifted down from the loft. I leaned over and whispered to Andy. "Do you think Hawkston will show up?"

He shrugged. "Well, he might. You'd think he'd want to investigate our witness claim. But he probably won't come alone. Cowards like him seldom do." He dug into his wood with the point of his knife.

A "Humph!" came from the loft and a trickle of straw drifted down. After much rustling around, Cook backed down the ladder, which creaked with every step. "I'd better go. Can't miss that meeting," he said, scratching his head as he stepped onto the ground. "If I leave now, I'll make it back just in time." He pointed up to the loft. "But Monroe is staying in case that Hawkston fellow decides to show. I know Monroe is young, but he's a strapping lad, a quick thinker and real handy with that Billy club of his."

****

It was well after 3:30 before old Fred Hawkston hobbled into the barn with another smaller, white-haired man trailing behind. Both had rifles tucked under their arms. When I saw the weapons, I bit my lip, thinking about the Billy club that young Monroe had for protection. "So, where's the party?" demanded Hawkston. He stopped in front of the large, smooth planked workbench and stared at Uncle Henry.

Andy's white-knuckled grip on his knife was the only outward sign that he'd heard as he focused on whittling the tip of this wood to a point.

"Don't look like much of a party," said the man with Fred as he glanced around. "Nothing but that white girl and a bunch of coons. I can't believe you dragged me away from the game for this, Fred."

"Relax, Lars, the party's just beginning," replied Fred, with one shaky hand pointing his shot-gun up at the loft.

170

I watched in horror as he jerked the trigger. Andy and I jumped at the gun blast, diving towards the ground.

"What do you think you're doing," shouted Uncle Henry as he put down his paintbrush and picked up a ballpeen hammer.

"Jesus, Fred!" hissed Lars through his teeth.

Oh my God! Hope he missed Monroe. Although straw trickled down after the shot, I didn't dare look up.

Fred roared with laughter. "Hey, did you hear something, Lars?" said Fred, cupping his hand around his ear. "I thought I heard a darky talk. But maybe I was mistaken." Then he turned towards me. "You, girl. Who's your precious witness? I hope you don't expect me to believe something one of these dumb niggers told you."

I could feel my face heating up. Rob had seen him, but he hadn't returned yet. *Time to change the subject.* "Back in 1912, you came out to this barn and murdered two young boys..."

"Now hold it right there," he interrupted, while he expelled the empty shotgun shell and loaded another in the barrel. "Who you talking about? You don't mean that German trash that lived here, do you?"

"You were seen here..." I started to say.

"Nobody saw nothing, girl," he interjected. "Sure, I come out here with my two cousins and had a chat with that Kraut farmer and his dumpy wife." He guffawed as he emphasized the "dumpy," the barrel of his gun drooping towards the ground. "Seems their delinquent boys stole something. I was dispatched here as an official deputy to investigate. I knew them boys had it but they wouldn't tell. Next day, they was all dead."

"You're denying you shot the boys?"

"'Course I didn't shoot them. They was both alive and well when I left," he insisted.

Uncle Henry's voice could barely be heard. "You shot the younger one in the belly. I saw you do it."

"You wasn't even there, boy."

"Oh, yes, I was. I worked here. I saw you shoot Phillip and you were the cause of Bruce falling from the loft. They might have been alive when you left here, but they both died that night. Their father did not shoot them." Uncle Henry looked directly at Fred. "Them boys died because of you. Bet you shot the parents too."

Fred stared at him for a moment, then burst out laughing. "You really don't think anyone will believe that cock-and-bull story, do you?"

"Henry Jackson was a witness and people will believe him," I said, standing stiff, my hands clenched at my sides.

"You going to tell, boy?" asked Fred. He wheeled around, faster than I thought possible for a man his age, and pointed his rifle at Henry.

"Time people knew the truth about the Strombergs," replied Henry.

Fred met Henry's gaze. "Maybe we should silence the black bird before he sings." His cackling outburst echoed throughout the barn.

Lars nudged Fred's arm that cradled his rifle. "Come on, Fred, let's get out of here. We don't need no trouble. Too many eyes around here," he said. "Besides, we come here to see the witness to that fire. Too dark in here for anybody

172

to recognize you then anyway. Seems it was just a ruse to get you out here. So let's skedaddle."

"Shut your fool mouth! Ain't nobody seen me here," snarled Fred. He jerked away from Lars and with both hands, raised his rifle waste high, his finger slipping into the trigger guard. "I come here to silence a witness and I mean to finish what I set out to do."

"Like you did them Strombergs?" Lars muttered.

"You weren't even here then!" retorted Fred. "Keep your pie-hole shut!"

"Well, all that big talk about taking out the witnesses sure got you kicked off the..."

"Shut up, you bastard!" screeched Fred, jamming his elbow into Lar's side. "Nobody can prove anything. Nobody!"

While his friend Lars doubled over in pain, Fred leveled his gun on Uncle Henry again. I opened my mouth to scream but could not utter even a sound as I watched Fred's finger touch the trigger.

"Duck, Uncle!" yelled Andy, lunging at Fred. Lars, who had stepped partly in front of Fred, sidestepped Andy's attack and brought the butt end of his rifle down on the backside of Andy's head as he passed by. The boy sprawled flat onto the floor at Fred's feet. Fred nudged Lars aside with his rifle barrel, then with his finger still on the trigger, pointed the gun at Andy's still body.

"No!" I screamed.

"Police! Stop, right where you are!" said Monroe from the loft. "You're under arrest." He slid down the rungs of the ladder and leaping to the floor, moved towards Fred and Lars, his wooden Billy club raised high.

"If you move one more step, I'll shoot this kid and then I'll shoot you. Don't be a fool," chuckled Fred. He locked eyes with Monroe but nodded towards Lars. "I can't believe the big policeman didn't even bring a gun."

"You can't shoot a cop, Fred. Come on, let's get out of here," hissed Lars.

"Hell, I'm 92 years old. I can shoot any damn cop I want. What are they going to do, put me away for life!" laughed Fred. "Why, they'll probably even give me a medal if I rid the world of a couple more useless niggers."

Monroe stopped in midstride, his club in ready position. His gaze was drawn to movement behind the workbench, followed by a clanking sound as if something metal had fallen to the ground.

Fred heard it too and approached the bench, pointing his rifle at the spot where Henry had been standing.

"Hey, come out from behind there, boy," he demanded.

Silence.

"Don't make me come back there and drag your sorry black ass out!" Fred shouted. He edged toward the bench, his rifle leveled. When he pulled the trigger, Lars, who stood several yards back, jumped, nearly dropping his own gun.

But before the boom had finished echoing through the rafters, the air was filled with child voices crying, "No! Stop!"

Everyone froze. The words seemed to spring from nowhere in particular.

"Huh? Who said that?" Fred's shark-eyes scanned the room. Only his ragged breathing broke the silence while bits of straw floated through the dusty light rays from above.

The haze from the expelled shell filled the air. I crouched behind the workbench with Uncle Henry, who put his fingers to his lips in a shushing motion, then motioned for me to follow as he crept to the side of the bench and peeked around. A board creaked and he halted.

The boys' voices rebounded off the wooden walls again. "Murderer! You killed our parents! You will pay."

"Who are you? Show yourself!" screamed Fred, a quiver in his voice as he spat out the words. He brandished his rifle as if he could scare them off. "You're afraid to be seen, aren't you?!"

A blurry vision of the two young boys appeared beside the post where the plane had been tied. The taller one spoke. "You shot them. You must pay."

"They would have told!" Fred insisted, a distinct shake in his voice.

The smaller figure mimicked, "You must pay."

"Pay! Pay! Pay!" they chanted.

Fred fumbled his rifle, leveling it on the transparent figures, and then pulling the trigger. The empty chamber clicked back. He looked down in horror at his gun. When he looked back up, the images had faded away. But before he could make a move, Monroe threw his club at Fred's gun, knocking it from his hand as he tackled the old man. Forcing Fred onto his belly, he sank one knee in the middle of his back and handcuffed the two gnarled hands together. Lars quickly dropped his rifle and raised his hands.

"You are under arrest for the attempted murders of Henry Jackson and Phillip Stromberg," said Monroe. Then he recited the rights to both men.

Lars's eyes were wild as he backed slowly towards the barn door. "Hey, I didn't even shoot my rifle. It was all his fault. He just wanted me to come in case he needed help. I didn't do any of it!"

Andy struggled to his feet, rubbing the back of his head.

Monroe shouted to him, "Hey, don't let Lars escape."

Lars turned and dashed for the open door. But before he could reach it, the portal slid shut. He collided with the door and fell to the ground. Scrambling to his feet, he heaved on the door but it wouldn't budge.

I smiled. Andy stared in amazement and continued to rub his head. "Don't worry, Andy," I said. "He won't be able to get out."

Lars continued to pull at the huge door while Andy calmly picked up his rifle and handed it to Monroe. "He won't need this anymore."

Andy cuffed Lars while Monroe went into the house to call for backup. About five minutes later, howling sirens filled the air along with the crunch of gravel as a police car, followed by an ambulance entered the yard. This time, I slid the door open with no problem. Andy and Monroe pushed handcuffed Lars and Fred out of the barn ahead of them towards the police car, which sat amidst a cloud of dust in the yard.

Chapter Nineteen

Justice

Both men were hustled off in the police car while Officer Monroe remained behind to talk further to Uncle Henry about the 1912 event. Andy, Auntie, Uncle Luther and I sat with Uncle Henry and Monroe at the dining table with mugs of fresh hot coffee and a plate of warm banana bread slices.

"Let me get this straight." Monroe opened his notebook and clicked his ball point pen. "Someone actually saw Fred set that fire the other night?"

Andy and I exchanged glances. "Well, Rob said he saw Fred light the fire and Jeb run from the barn afterwards," I told him with hesitation, knowing he'd never believe that two ghosts saw Fred set the fire. "Fred must have told Lars about the fire, because Lars mentioned it out in the barn. I'm really not clear as to why Jeb was involved with Fred in wanting to burn the barn down, though."

"Well, it looks like Lars did us all a big favor, doesn't it?" said Monroe. "We heard what he said. I think that after some questioning, Fred will reveal his motive for setting the fire. But you must tell me who this Rob fellow is. Where has he gone?"

I shrugged. "Good question. He told us he was here to investigate Jeb Bracken, who has been following me around since before I actually got here. But Rob has been gone since yesterday. He seemed to know quite a bit about the Strombergs too, but I'm not sure why he cares about that."

"Interesting," said Monroe, jotting in his spiral notebook. "Now, back to the events concerning the Strombergs."

177

He turned towards Uncle Henry. "Even if you testify that you saw Fred and his cousins back in 1912, there's no proof that you were there if no one actually saw you. Do you have anything that proves you were there that night? I'm not sure we can prosecute him for the shooting of young Phil or hold him responsible for Bruce's death or the death of their parents on only the hearsay of Lars."

Henry dunked a corner of his bread in his steaming coffee. "Well, there is the letter," he said.

"That's right! The letter!" I exclaimed, putting down my slice without taking a bite. "Andy showed it to me at college. That's how I knew you'd worked with Gustave Whitehead."

Uncle Henry looked from me to Andy then back to me.

"What letter is that, Dad?" asked Auntie.

"I don't know if it means anything," Uncle Henry said, "but I wrote a letter that I meant to leave with Mr. Whitehead before I left town, but I didn't. I put it in the old family Bible." Then he turned to Auntie, "But it seems young Andy found it."

"I just borrowed it to look up about Gustave White-head," said Andy. "I came across it by mistake one day when I was leafing through the Bible. I have it up in my room, Uncle. I'll go up and get it." He nearly tripped over the chair leg as he pushed away from the table. "Oh, sorry," he muttered. Sprinting through the living room he took the stairs, two at a time. In less than a minute, he was back, out of breath, beaming as he thrust the folded paper at Uncle.

Henry perused the sheet and nodded his head. "Yes, this is it. Look, it is dated August 3rd, the day the Strombergs died in 1912. This should prove I was there the night

178

before when the boys hid the plane, the night Fred and his cronies attacked the family. No one else knew about the plane. In fact," he said, pausing to look at the note again before continuing, "I came back and bought this property because of the plane stored in the barn. Nobody wanted the farm because they thought it was haunted, so it sat empty for almost 25 years before I bought it and fixed it up."

Uncle Luther chuckled and shook his head. "So that's why you were so desperate to keep this old farm in the family. And here I thought all the time that you were just being generous."

Auntie pointed to the note in Henry's hand. "You know I found that slip of paper years ago and was going to ask you about it, but forgot." She sat back in her chair with a smug smile and folded her arms. "It's a good thing I put it back in there. I never open that Bible anyway, since I got that new updated version."

"Will you read the letter to us?" asked Monroe.

Henry stared at it a moment, then began. "'Dear Mr. Whitehead. I hope you won't be mad when you find out about Phil and Bruce taking No. 22. They done it so it wouldn't get burnt up with the other things those men took from you and got killed for their trouble. I hear people say you lost that trial because you was a German person and people are afraid of you. It's not fair. I know where No. 22 is because I watched the boys hide it. It is safe and I won't tell no one.'" He cleared his throat before continuing, "'I'm really going to miss working at your shop but I have to go away for a while.'"

Henry laid the paper down, staring at the large fern filling the corner across from where he sat. Then, he spoke so quietly that I could barely hear him. "I had just talked to Mr. Stromberg who had told me that the boys were dead and he was going away for a spell." His hands encircled his coffee cup and stared down at it. "I was in the barn collect-

179

ing my things and stuffed the note in the Bible when I heard someone coming. It was Fred and the two men from the night before. They'd come back to talk to Mr. Stromberg again about the plane. I was outside when I heard two rifle shots. I don't know what happened after that because I took off. I guess from what Lars said, Fred and his cronies shot the Strombergs to keep them quiet."

"Why didn't you tell the police?" asked Monroe.

Henry looked sharply at Monroe. "It's just like Fred said. Nobody would believe a negro boy then..." His shoulders sagged and his voice cracked, "or maybe even now."

Monroe shook his head. "Mr. Jackson, they'll believe you. Times have changed." He leaned across the table looking directly into his eyes. "I believe you."

Henry's eyes softened. "I appreciate that, sir." He glanced down and refolded the note.

"I was just wondering," began Monroe, looking from person to person. "Whatever happened to Mr. Whitehead after you left?"

"I heard he continued with various inventions but because of his injured eye and heart problems, he didn't pursue his flying dream," explained Uncle Henry, popping into his mouth the last bite of his banana bread and wiping his mouth with his napkin.

"So, if he didn't do any more flying, what did he do?" asked Monroe.

"I read how he entered a competition for a prize in New York concerning developing a safety device for trains. He and another electrical engineer friend developed a "third-rail" safety device whereby a brush under the engine would

180

cause the train to stop when coming into contact with the third rail."

Henry paused, emptying his coffee cup. He was considerably more animated as he told us about Whitehead's achievements. "I heard that the last work he did was to invent a concrete laying machine to help lay out the road up on Long Hill, outside Bridgeport. They say it was the first known automatic machine of its kind." He smiled and shook his head. "The man sure had a way with engines and machines."

"How long did Mr. Whitehead live?" asked Uncle Luther.

"I think he passed on in 1927, almost broke, from what I heard. They buried him in a pauper's grave," sighed Henry. "Left his family with only that house up on the hill and eight dollars."

Monroe wrote out a statement right then and there and had Uncle Henry read and sign it, along with witness signatures from Uncle Luther and me. Auntie must have mentioned to Monroe about Uncle Henry's tendency to suddenly move on without even saying goodbye. After Uncle Henry signed the paper, he smiled at me and nodded. "Justice will finally be served."

****

That evening, I was tired and sad as I packed my suitcase, readying myself for the trip back to Illinois on Wednesday. *I've come all this way and been so close to getting proof of Gustave Whitehead's successful flight and now I have to go back empty-handed. Andy and I searched the barn for the photo, but it's gone. What am I going to tell the editor? He'll throw out the story of the flights on August 14th, 1901 with no photo proof. It won't matter that there were two newspapers that covered the event. Without that picture of his plane in flight, no one will believe either of those articles. I glanced through the Stella Randolph book at the witnesses' accounts with signed affidavits attached even though no one believed them. At least I have Uncle Henry's tape recorded interviews about all those times he'd helped launch the flights---both successful and unsuccessful. Gustave Whitehead deserves a prominent place in aviation history, instead of being ignored and discredited outside of Connecticut.* I tried to fold my slippery light nylon jacket but frustration won out and I ended up just jamming it into a corner of the suitcase. *It just isn't fair.*

I will write that article anyway. There are all of the other materials from the briefcase and if I can contact Rob concerning his photos of the plane before it was destroyed, that will help make my case. How strange that he has left so suddenly.

****

The next morning I was up and dressed early. With suitcase in hand, I crept down the stairs just as the grandfather clock bonged six times. The smell of freshly perked coffee permeated the air as I dragged my heavy bag into the kitchen. Auntie bustled about, frying bacon and scrambling eggs, the radio in the background softly playing "Happy Together."

"Good morning. You didn't have to get up to feed me," I said.

"Good morning, yourself. Do you think I would let you leave on your trip with an empty stomach?" Auntie filled a plate and put it at the place already set at the kitchen table. "Now, you sit right down here and get a good start to your day."

I smiled and sat. "Thanks. This is wonderful."

As I ate, the newscaster interrupted the song. "I was just handed a special bulletin from the newsroom. There has been a fatal accident at the edge of Bridgeport where a black Fury, ran off the bridge and sank in the river. People in a VW bus, driving behind him, witnessed the tragedy. Shep Greene, driver of the bus said, 'I don't know what was wrong with the dude. He whizzed past us just up the road, then suddenly swerved too much and ran right off the side. Surfside and George, here, leaped out and tried to save him. But they couldn't get the door open. Man, I guess the guy was slumped in the driver's seat, so maybe he had a heart attack or something.' More details on this accident at 8:00."

"Oh, my gosh! It was Jeb!" I said. "He was still around. And that bus—Shep and George were two of the guys who helped me escape from Jeb in the warehouse. I'm sure glad they weren't hurt."

Auntie clucked her tongue and shook her head. "Thank heaven for that, at least."

It's too bad about Jeb, but I just can't muster much sympathy for him. At least he won't be lurking around anymore corners after me. I put down my fork and picked up my empty plate. "Is Uncle Henry up yet?"

"Well, of course. He rises with the birds---bright and early. But, I'm afraid you've missed him. He left earlier this morning."

"What do you mean, 'left'?"

"Why he packed up and skedaddled. He never lets anyone know when he decides to leave."

"Where does he go when he leaves?"

Auntie shook her head. "He refuses to tell us, but I think he had a small cabin down in the Blue Ridge Mountains. He has a phone down there and did at least give me the number where he could be reached in case of an emergency. But he made me promise never to call him there unless it was really important. He always comes back for holidays, but he is a very private man and I have to respect that. I hope someday, when he knows he cannot survive on his own, that he'll come back here for good."

"I wish I could have told him goodbye," I said.

"Don't you worry about it, child. You know, I've never seen him take to a body like he took to you. Why, by the way he smiled when you came into the room, I could tell that he trusted you. I've never seen him open up and talk to anyone so much. You're very special, Lorie." Auntie reached down and gave me a hug.

These are wonderful folks. I don't even think of them as colored people anymore – they're more like my family. I'm really going to miss them, I thought as I waved goodbye that day.

Chapter Twenty

Blindsided

Home at last. The streetlights just flicked on as I pulled into my driveway. *6:37 and my stomach is growling. The trip back was uneventful, thank goodness. But now comes the hardest job of all—writing the article.* After sliding out from the driver's seat, I stretched and breathed in the fragrant, flower-scented air. *There will be time to deal with that tomorrow.*

I struggled up onto the front porch, my arms heaped with maps, the Stella Randolph book, and a paper bag of trash that was in the passenger seat. After unlocking the door, I kicked aside the small pile of mail that had collected under the slot and dumped the load onto the kitchen table before heading back for the suitcase.

Heaving it on my bed, I flopped down beside it with arms outstretched and eyes closed. *It sure is good to be home, but, lying here won't get stuff done.* I sighed as I pushed myself up and off the bed. Flipping the suitcase latches open, the lid sprang up revealing a dense mound of crunched clothes. I took one look at it. *Later! It's not going anywhere.*

Back at the kitchen table, I sank into the chair and carefully unwrapped the half-sandwich I'd saved from earlier that day. I sifted through the stack of mail as I chewed, pulling out a small, stiff, manila envelope with the return address of Bridgeport, post-marked only two days earlier. *What in the world could I have forgotten?* I slid a paring knife under the flap and slit it open. A folded piece of cardboard was jammed tightly inside. After much tugging and pulling, I finally sliced through the envelope itself. The cardboard square tumbled out onto the table.

185

When I picked up the cardboard, a photograph dropped to the table from between its folds. Holding the faded picture by its edges, I stared at the scalloped-winged airplane, with Whitehead as pilot, flying several feet above the ground. *Oh my God!* A small scrap of paper clung to its back for a moment before fluttering down on top of the other mail. I leaned over and read it out loud:

"Lorie, I found this photo among my paint containers in the barn and knew you would want it. Please take good care of it. There has been no sign of 'the boys' so they must be satisfied that justice was served. Thank you for all you did to free them from their anguish and bring out the truth. Fred H. was arrested and the trial will be in about 6 months. Henry A. Jackson."

With the old briefcase of papers and this photo, there's enough proof to write the article! If only I had those pictures Rob took before the plane was destroyed. They just have to exist! I must find a way to contact him.

****

I spent the entire next day organizing the material and making notes. At noon, I took a break and drove the picture and some of the other drawings and snapshots to a photo lab to have two sets of duplicates made. That way, I could include a set with my article and keep a copy for myself. Back home, I settled in and wrote the actual article in a couple of hours. Satisfied with the rough draft, I took time out to jot a note to Auntie explaining what Uncle Henry had sent me and promising to return all the Whitehead originals when I was finished with them. *After all, they were found on Uncle Henry's property, so they really belonged to him or perhaps to the museum in Bridgeport.*

It was late afternoon when I opened a can of Corned Beef Hash and heated it on the stove. As I stirred it, I pondered how I could find Rob. The phone number Officer Cook had given me turned out to be another dead end. However, my shared memory with Rob of Paradise, where I had vacationed, gave me an idea. While the hash sizzled in the pan, I dialed the number that the information operator had given me for the General Store in Paradise.

I smiled at Mrs. Berns' delightful, "Hiddee-ho!" when she answered.

Tucking the phone on my left shoulder while I dished up the hash, I couldn't help grinning at the memories her voice conjured. We chatted for a few minutes before I brought up the reason I was calling. "I'm looking for that fellow who worked for you years ago: Rob Gutierrez."

"Unfortunately," replied Mrs. Berns, "the Gutierrez family left the area, oh, about 10 years ago. I think they went back East somewhere."

"Oh," I said.

Mrs. Berns must have heard the disappointment in my voice. "I wish I could tell you more."

We chatted a few moments and I promised if I was ever visiting the Upper Peninsula, I'd be sure to stop in, before I thanked her and hung up. Suddenly the steaming hash didn't look so appealing and after only a few bites, I ended up covering it with foil and jamming it into the refrigerator. *"Gutierrez" is a far too common name to just start looking in phone books, especially in the vast Washington D.C. area.* I stared at the rough draft of my article as it lay on the kitchen table.

A hard knock at the door made me jump. *That's probably Ben. He told me yesterday he'd be over today to proofread the article.* I glanced through the small window and saw a tall figure dressed in a long rain coat and hat with

187

his back to me. Why is he so dressed up on such a beautiful spring day? I flipped the dead-bolt and pulled open the door.

The figure turned towards me and stepped over the threshold before I could stop him. Then he threw his hat on the table and grabbed me in a tight hug.

"Rob! What are you doing here?"

His spicy scent filled my head as he grasped my shoulders and pushed me at arms' length, grinning. "Lorie, you look wonderful!"

Words completely left me as I gazed up into those stunning blue eyes. "I was just trying to find a number for you!"

"Well, you can quit looking. I'm right here!"

"Exactly why are you here?" I asked, my voice suddenly hoarse.

"Actually, two reasons." *His teeth glisten when he smiles.* "First, I wanted to see you again. I couldn't stop thinking about you." I melted into the warmth of his embrace as he stroked my hair. "You look so good," he purred in my ear.

I can't let him do this to me. I pulled away and stood behind a chair that was pushed in at the kitchen table, putting a barrier between us. *There are too many unanswered questions to be sucked into this emotional moment.* "You said there were two reasons you came. So, what is the other reason?"

"Well, my boss wanted me to collect those papers you found from the airplane rubble," said Rob. My astounded look prompted him to add, "I'm prepared to pay you a reasonable amount to release them to me."

"Exactly who is your boss? And why would he be interested in the Whitehead materials?" I demanded.

"He's connected with the Museum," he said, through those perfect teeth. "I thought you knew that."

"I knew you weren't interested in Jeb. I'll bet you two were working together, weren't you?"

His silence was answer enough for me. I took a step back.

"I suppose it doesn't matter that I kept Jeb from really hurting you, does it?" he said, more as a statement than a question.

I glared. "Your boss can't be interested in the papers for a display at the Museum. Not after what I heard about that Contract with the Wright Brothers. What exactly do they propose to do with the Whitehead papers?"

"You know the Museum has thousands of artifacts which are not displayed. They simply want to preserve any historical aeronautical materials available. I'd think that would be what you'd want. If they are not properly dealt with, those papers will crumble and disintegrate over time." Rob reached towards me, but I managed to keep the chair between us.

"I found those papers. And Uncle Henry's family told me I could have them for the article. I plan on returning them when I'm done with them. After all, they were found in his barn."

"But the Museum will be able to preserve them so much more efficiently and they'll be safe," he insisted.

"But your Museum will not display anything of Gustave Whitehead's because of that stupid Contract!"

"Well, that may be the case. But you have to admit, they know a lot more about preservation of old documents than you do," he countered.

I gripped the chair so hard my hands began to ache and looked hard at Rob. "What's the use of preserving them if the Museum is going to pack them away where no one can see them?"

He dug into his back pocket and pulled out a silver money clip packed with bills. "So, how much are they worth to you?"

"They're not for sale," I snapped.

"Let me put it this way: either I pay you for the papers or I just take them. I'm prepared to do either." Those stunning blue eyes turned to ice.

"But you took pictures of the papers, didn't you? And what about those photos from the airplane, before it was destroyed?" I reminded him.

He laughed. "There are no pictures. That was all for show."

I pulled the chair closer to me, as if it might leap away from me at any moment. The ringing phone burst the tension in the room. As I lunged to answer it, my foot caught on the chair leg and flipped the chair onto its side. Ignoring it, I grabbed the receiver and took a deep breath.

"Hello!" I yelled, expelling all my air.

"Hey, Lorie, what's going on?"

"Oh, Ben, I'm sorry. I didn't mean to yell at you." I glared at Rob, standing silently nearby.

"Is your article done? Can I come over and read it now?"

"Oh, that's OK. I'll be here."

Ben's voice was suddenly urgent. "Hey, are you OK?"

I almost stuttered my reply. "Oh, by the way---how about those Tigers?"

"You're in trouble, aren't you? Don't worry, I'm on my way!" Then the dial tone droned in my ear.

"See you later," I said and hung up.

"So what was that all about?" asked Rob, eying me with suspicion.

"Oh, he was due to come over today, but won't be able to make it. You see, he's polite, not like some people I know who come barging into your house and demanding things."

His eyes glistened with amusement. "So, what was that bit about tigers?"

"Not that it's any of your business, but the Tigers are a baseball team. We're both big fans."

He shook his head and shrugged his shoulders, taking a seat at the table. "I don't suppose you have any coffee?"

"No. It's gone and I have things to do. Please leave."

With a damp sponge in hand, I turned away from him and began wiping down the counters and the refrigerator with gusto.

"I'm not leaving without the papers," he said. "Now if you want to be rid of me, just hand them over." The money clip clanked onto the table. "I'm authorized to give you up to $500.00 for them. There's the whole amount---in cash."

I ignored him and sprinkled scouring powder into the sink. *Wow, that is a lot of cash. He must need them really bad to offer that much.*

"Or I can take your place apart searching for them," he said. "I'll find them if they're here." The hard tone of his threat made it hard for me to swallow. Out of the corner of my eye I watched as he wandered out of the kitchen and down the hall. I heard him in the bathroom, then the bedroom. Doors and drawers opened and closed. The soft rustling of things moving around piqued my curiosity. So, I dried my hands, tiptoed to the bedroom door and peered around the corner. Rob was rummaging through the dresser drawers. Surprisingly, the room was as I had left it. Nothing had been tossed on the floor or strewn about the room. *Thank God!* Satisfied that he was searching in a civilized manner, I returned to the kitchen and the sink. *I could call the police, but he really hasn't done anything to harm me...yet. No, he won't hurt me.*

Rob sighed when he stepped through the doorway almost ten minutes later. Through the stillness, I could feel him staring at me.

"They're not here," I said without turning around.

He moved close behind me and I felt his breath on my neck. "Then where are they?"

"Safe."

He grasped my shoulders and spun me around to face him. "Where?" he hissed.

"In town. Safe." I barely uttered the words when he raised his hand as if to hit me.

"Tell me where!"

A knock at the door diverted his attention long enough for me to pull away from his grip. I ran to the door and flung it open. "Ben! Boy am I glad to see you!" I grabbed his arm and yanked him inside.

"What's wrong?"

"Thank God you came!" I pointed towards the kitchen. "He's in there trying to make me tell him where the Whitehead papers are."

"Who?"

I dashed back into the kitchen, but the room was empty, the back door stood open and the money clip with the cash was gone.

I slammed the door shut and threw the dead bolt, then ran back into the living room and locked that door as well. Ben stood puzzled watching me whirl through the house, locking all the windows. When I returned, breathless, I explained about Rob trying to buy the papers for the Museum and his trying to make me tell him where they were. I just knew that Rob would not leave me alone until he had them, so I scribbled a note on a scrap of paper and thrust it at Ben.

"Here, go to the photo store and give the owner this message. His name is Chad. I'll take off the other way to the Laundromat. Call me when you pick them up. Rob doesn't know you yet and probably won't know to follow you." Ben agreed as I grabbed up a bag of dirty laundry. We peered out the windows and finding the street empty, both left in opposite directions.

The Laundromat, Grocery store, cleaners, and gas station trip went off without a hitch. Although there was no sign of anyone following me, I was still edgy when I pulled back into my driveway. *I have no idea what Rob's car looks like, but I'm pretty sure no one has followed me.* The phone was ringing as I unlocked the back door.

Stepping in, I dropped the bag of groceries on the counter and flung the dry-cleaning across the kitchen chair, then picked up the phone. "Hello!"

Ben talked so fast that I had to stop him and have him repeat what he'd said. "I didn't think I'd been followed to the photo shop but just before I left, a dark, curly-haired man came in behind me. It was lucky that I had given Chad the slip of paper before that guy came in. Chad said he thought the whole thing sounded too Secret Agentish, but he agreed to do it. The stranger left the shop just as I got into my car and started the engine. Then I waited and followed his black Cadillac to the Village Inn Motel at the edge of town. Lorie, I'm sure this guy was Rob. Listen, I gotta go now. I'm late for an appointment."

"Thanks Ben. But you be careful. If he shows up at your place, call me and remember our Tigers code. Don't trust him. Do you know anyone at the police station?"

"As a matter of fact, I do. My roommate Frank's cousin, Josh Brannon, is a deputy down there. Why?"

"Well, would you mind calling him and alerting him about Rob? I think he could be dangerous if he can't get the papers soon. I know Josh can't do anything until Rob makes a move, but at least he could be aware of the situation," I suggested.

"OK. That's a good idea. But do you really think he'd hurt us just for some stupid papers? I don't think he did anything to Chad while he was there. He really didn't have

194

time. He came out of there only a couple of minutes after I did."

"Don't be fooled," I said. "I think he's more dangerous than he looks."

****

The next day, Saturday, after a trip to the dry cleaner's in the morning, I had barely come through the door around noon when the phone rang. "Lorie. Chad from the photo store. I got some good news and some bad. The old photos and papers you brought in? Well, someone broke in here last night and stole the copies we had out drying. That's all I can find that's missing. The good news is we still have the originals locked away along with the negatives. I'll go ahead and make more copies. Do you still want me to mail them?"

"Yes! Throw those originals in the mail today along with the negatives you took! I'll have Ben come in to pick up the copies with a note from me. If anyone else asks you anything about them, just say they were all stolen. OK? Don't mention anything about the originals." He chuckled but agreed.

When I hung up, the phone rang again. I snatched up the receiver. "Hello?" There was a long pause and it sounded like someone breathing on the other end. Then the phone clicked and there was nothing but dial tone. *Is someone checking to see if I'm home? But why is he still following me? After all, he now has the papers he came for.*

While I toured the house, checking the locks on the doors and windows, I decided that I should call Brad Peters and make an appointment to present the article to him. The sooner the article was finished and in other hands, the safer

I'd be. If Chad mailed the originals today, they'd be here in tomorrow's delivery.

"Hello, Brad?" I said with a slight hoarseness in my voice. "Remember that article about the guy who flew before the Wright Brothers? Well, it's almost finished. When can we get together?" He hemmed and hawed but finally agreed to see me Monday afternoon at 4:45.

Just before I hung up, there was a strange click as if someone had been on an extension in the other room. There were no other phones in the house, so I suspected someone had bugged my phone. *It could have been done when I'd been gone over Easter. If Rob has indeed been listening in, then he knows about the originals still at the photo store and my appointment on Monday. I have to talk to Ben. He'll go with me.* Rather than call him on my phone, I decided to hop in my car and drive over to his place. Ben looked up and down the street for any suspicious cars after I had stepped through the front door. Then he threw the bolt drew the drapes in his living room.

"You really think your phone was bugged?" he asked.

"Well, there was this weird click when the call was disconnected and I've watched enough Mission: Impossible and Man from U.N.C.L.E. to know when a phone is bugged or not."

I had never seen Ben so serious. "Did you unscrew the earpiece and check it out?"

"No...but I played it safe and came here to talk to you in person rather than call you."

"So, what's up?"

"Would you be free after work Monday at 4:30 to go with me to see the guy about my article? I think our friend

Rob might show up there. Oh, and would you stop by the photo shop later today to pick up the copies of the papers?"

****

The rest of the day was spent writing and editing the article. Now, with the photo in my possession, the article seemed to write itself. The first draft was done by 4:00 and after Ben delivered the copies of the documents, I sifted through them, inserting them in strategic places in the article. With Ben's help, we had the whole thing done and ready for the final typing by 6:30 that evening.

"Come on, Lorie, let's take a break and check out the new pizza place over on 5th Street," suggested Ben. "I hear it's an old English Pub style place and they even have a live band on Saturdays."

"Oh, I don't know. I'm really worn out. I don't know if I'm ready for the dance scene tonight."

"Come on," he urged. "It'll do us both good to get out and relax. I promise not to make you dance."

"Well, I guess we gotta eat sometime, right?"

Ben laughed and held my coat as I shrugged into it, as he sang a rendition of the McDonald's commercial, "You deserve a break today—so get up and get away to...the pizza place!"

****

Sunday should have been a day of rest. However, with work starting again Monday and laundry to do and the final typing of the article, there was little time to relax. Ben

197

was off at church, singing in their choir for Sunday services, so I was on my own today. I threw on a couple of records and did a whirlwind housecleaning tour before digging back into the article. I know I probably spent too long studying that photo of Whitehead in his plane, but the whole idea fascinated me. *What I would have given to have seen that happen! Uncle Henry was one lucky fellow to have witnessed those events and known such a great man. How could people have overlooked such genius back then? So what if he was a German. His passion was flying and building engines so others could fly and that should be recognized. It doesn't matter what his nationality was. History can really be changed if I can just get this article accepted and published.*

****

Monday afternoon, Ben and I climbed up the long staircase from the street, above a sporting goods store, to Brad Peters' office. Three other people occupied offices down the hall from his. We entered through the door labeled, "Brad Peters, Editor" in big block letters, at precisely 4:45, stepping into a small room lined with bookshelves and a giant oak desk. One could look down from a large window onto the street below, where a string of cars slowed for the stoplight.

After shaking hands and introductions, we were directed to two chairs across from the desk. I unhooked the string around the fastener on the manila envelope and pulled out the article and photos, handing them to Brad. He rocked back in his swivel chair, propping one foot on the edge of his desk, and scanned the article. His light brown hair, which had probably been combed neatly when he'd arrived in the morning, dangled across his forehead, brushing his eyebrows as he read. When he removed his foot and slid forward, resting both elbows on the desk, the unbuttoned collar of his white short-sleeved shirt hung cockeyed. The knot on his thin maroon tie had been pulled down from his neck and a streak of black along the edge of his arm looked as if he'd been leaning on a newspaper. He stared at the photographs, slowly checking each one, and laying them upside down next to the article.

"Well, it looks like a pretty complete account. I'm a little unsure about this picture, though," he said, pulling the in-flight one aside. "The 1902 date written on here does not correspond with your 1901 claim to flight."

"I realize that," I said, standing and pointing to the photo. "I think it was taken somewhat later, but with the 1902 date, it still precedes the Wright Brothers' 1903 flight, so it is well worth including. Besides, there were two different accounts of White-head's 1901 flight from newspapers along with several eyewitness accounts, so that should be enough proof."

I glanced out the window down at the street as a large black Cadillac pulled up on the opposite side, nodding to Ben to look out the window.

Brad slowly shook his head. "Well, I don't know. I promised you I'd show it to my boss and I will, but I can't guarantee he'll print it. If I were you, I'd just use your first initial and last name. That way no one will know it was written by a woman."

I jammed my hands onto my hips. "But..." I started, pausing when Ben elbowed me in the side and jerked his head towards the window.

"He's here!" hissed Ben. "Don't let him in!"

"Who's here?" asked Peters. Someone thudded up the outside stairs followed by a loud knock on the door.

"Come in!" Brad shouted from his desk, keeping his eyes on us.

Rob stepped through the doorway, looking directly at Brad, not acknowledging Ben or me. "Brad Peters? I need to discuss an issue of importance with you. And bring along that article on your desk." He then looked at me, his gaze cold and defiant. "Government business. In private. In the hall."

Brad raised one eyebrow and shrugged at me before rising from his desk. "I'll only be a minute," he said, following Rob out of the office, my article clutched in his hand.

I started after him. "But my article!"

"I'll only be a moment. Stay here," insisted Peters.

Ben peeked into the hall, hoping to hear what was being said, but they had walked all the way to the far end and were talking with their backs to us in low voices. Five minutes passed before Brad's return, alone and empty-handed. He told me Rob had left through the "Exit" door lit up at that end of the hall.

He shook his head. "I'm sorry, Lorie, but I can't accept your article."

I couldn't believe me ears. "But why? I don't understand. And where is my article?"

Chapter Twenty-One

Rob

"Oh, I'm sorry but Gutierrez took it from me and said he'd get it back to you. Good thing the photos were still on my desk. You did make a carbon copy of it, didn't you?" He handed me the manila folder. "I take it you know this Gutierrez fellow. He's says the Government has an interest in keeping this whole Whitehead matter quiet. He didn't elaborate, but told me he had tried to convince you to give it up," Brad said with a shrug. "There would be no point in even showing it to my boss if there's a chance of a hassle with the feds. I've got my own job to consider, you know."

I jumped up from my chair. "Sure Rob wants to keep the Whitehead matter quiet. Did he tell you he works for the Smithsonian? That's the 'government' that he was talking about. It's the Museum that is afraid they'll lose their precious Kitty Hawk display if there is any proof that someone flew before the Wrights. As I stated in my article, the Contract is a fact that can't be changed and shouldn't be hidden from the public." I felt my face flush hot. "After all, we Americans have a right to know the truth about our own aviation history."

"Even if I were to take this article to my boss, he'd pass on it because, as Gutierrez pointed out, the Museum has too much power and money to fight it. Personally, I think you are right in wanting this to go public, but you'll have to find another place to get it published," said Brad. "There must be some underground newspaper that would love to print it."

"Yes, there probably is. But if it is put out underground, very few people will see it. I want visibility. This is aviation history we're talking about. Besides, Gustave Whitehead deserves more."

Ben stood beside me. "Hey, maybe the Times would print it." I turned to him and glared but that didn't seem to faze him. "Bridgeport isn't that far from New York City," he continued, "and if the Governor of Connecticut believes in Whitehead, maybe the Times will accept it. After all, they are bigger and have more money behind them than most magazines."

"I suppose it might be worth a try," I shook my head. *They just don't understand.* I turned and put out my hand to Brad. "Thanks anyway, for your time."

He grasped it and held on. "Hey, it is a well written article, Lorie. I hope he'll get it back to you. You can use me as a reference if you need to."

They clomped down the stairs to the street. It wasn't until we reached my car that Ben spoke. "I still don't trust that Rob guy. I think you'd better guard those photos and negatives carefully until you find a publisher."

He opened the driver's door for me. As I stepped into the car, I whispered, "I don't trust him either. That's why I've got an idea where to put them where he'll never think to look." Jamming the manila envelope with the pictures under the front seat, I stuffed a folded up blanket on top of them. "I'm sure we haven't seen the last of him."

****

The next morning was overcast but warm. I glanced up at the cloud-choked sun. *Looks like it will rain again today.* I hurried through the parking lot towards the Library. Mrs. Comstock was true to form when I stepped through the front door two minutes past the hour. "I do not tolerate late, young lady," she scowled. "You'll stay five minutes longer before taking lunch today."

202

To keep from rolling my eyes, I swallowed hard and focused on my desk, piled high with new books. Well, at least I'll be able to keep busy, which helps the time pass quicker. I stripped the plastic cover from my typewriter and flipped the power switch.

Someone at the front desk cleared his throat. "How was your spring vacation?"

To my delight, Professor Meinz leaned over the front desk, his voice barely above a whisper. "I heard you went back east. You have family back there?"

I stepped up to the desk busying myself with straightening the pencils and rearranging the stamp and blank paper pads. "No, no family there. I went to research for an article I'm writing. So how was your vacation?"

"Just fine. We took the kids into Chicago for a long weekend, to the museums and all before heading out to my folks for a week on the farm," he replied. "Perhaps you can assist me in finding something about this author."

He scribbled a name down on the blank pad. I glanced at the name and said, "Be glad to! Always love getting away from my desk for a while."

I led the way to the card catalog and thumbed through it. The front door swished open and out of the corner of my eye, a tall figure in the raincoat and hat entered. I thought nothing of it until I heard the man's Spanish accent. *What is Rob doing here?*

"Can somebody help me?"

I stepped behind the card catalog and grabbed up a large book that had been set on top of it. Holding it in front of my face, I peered around it, as Mrs. Comstock bustled from her office and spoke to him in a low voice. Then to my horror, Mrs. Comstock's gaze scanned the library and stopped on Prof. Meinz. She pointed right at us. I set the book down and hurried off into the stacks, where I could watch without being seen. Taking the hint from my sudden departure, Professor Meinz stepped out in front of Rob as he headed towards me. "What's the rush?"

Pushing him aside, Rob snapped, "Out of my way. I need to talk to Lorie."

I wove through the rows of books towards the stairwell, just as he appeared at the far end of the stacks, trotting towards me, with Professor Meinz and Mrs. Comstock rounding the corner behind him. I tore up the steps two at a time, my shoes clanking on the metal stairs, nearly colliding with Ben standing by the 2nd floor railing.

"Ben, go call your police friend now. Rob's here," I said, sucking in air between every few words. "I'll try to keep him busy. Take the elevator down and use the phone in Mrs. Comstock's office."

"But Lorie, I can't leave you..." he started.

"Just go! And hurry!" I darted off between the walls of books, peeking through the bare spots on the shelves.

Rob crested the stairs and grabbed Ben's arm. "Where did she go?"

Ben shook his head and tried to pull away. "I don't know. Why are you chasing her?"

"Tell me, where did she go?" He jerked Ben around and raised his hand to slap him. Another hand blocked his.

Professor Meinz stepped in front of Rob, nose to nose with him. "You leave him alone! What do you want with Lorie?"

204

"Out of my way," Rob demanded, his accent more pronounced than ever. "It's a personal matter between her and me. None of your business."

Professor Meinz clenched his teeth and stood his ground. "Well, I'm making it my business."

Rob's tone was suddenly gracious and he smiled as if there was nothing wrong. "I merely want to speak with her. I have an article she wrote and wish to return to her and she has something of mine I must collect. Now, I'm on a tight schedule, so if you'll excuse me---." He tried to shove the Professor aside but Meinz would not budge.

Mrs. Comstock had caught up with the two men. She glared at Rob. "Then you may deal with Lorie when she is not at work. You will not disturb my library."

"When will she be leaving?"

She straightened her back and glared at him. "She will be taking her lunch break near noon."

I watched Ben gape in horror at Mrs. Comstock. Rob turned and jogged down the stairs. Mrs. Comstock stepped in front of Ben. "Come directly to my office," she demanded. Then she pulled Professor Meinz aside and said something quietly to him.

I crept up behind Ben, who was staring out over the railing towards the front door and whispered in his ear, "At least he's gone, for now, anyway. I think Mrs. Comstock scared him away."

Ben jumped, nearly upending the books on the cart beside him. "She wants to see me in her office. I can't believe she told him when you'd be going for lunch! I wonder what she wants to see me for. What did I do?"

205

"I'll walk down with you," I insisted.

We all went back down stairs to the front desk. Mr. Meinz broke away towards the card catalog again and Ben headed into Mrs. Comstock's office.

There was no way I was going to sit at my desk until I knew what was going on. So, I groped in the pockets of my coat, which hung on the hook just outside the office entrance, for a fictitious scrap of paper; their voices, hushed but distinct.

"Now, Ben, I want you to stick close to Lorie when you go for lunch. If she goes to the restroom, you wait outside the door for her. If she waits in line at the cafeteria, you wait with her. Do you under-stand? That person who was in here looking for her is not to be trusted," said Mrs. Comstock. *I can't believe she's actually worried about me.*

"That's what I planned on doing anyway. Would it be all right if I used your phone to alert a friend of mine from the police department?" asked Ben.

"Do you really think that's necessary?"

"Well, the guy is suspected of robbing a local photo shop and has already threatened Lorie once. I think it's time for the police to intervene," Ben insisted.

"Yes, you may make the call. Then, it's back to work."

Mrs. Comstock's shoes clacked on the floor as she stood up, so I hurried back to my desk. Rolling a blank card into the typewriter, I opened a new book. Mrs. Comstock's door opened and she sailed past me, not even glancing my way.

****

206

At 12:06, there was no sign of Rob when Ben and I left the library and headed for the Union. All during lunch, things were quiet, but tense. We talked little, spending most of the time scanning the room. Relieved that Rob was nowhere in sight, we headed back for work.

At precisely 12:29, Ben opened the library door for me. "I can't believe he'd give up that easily."

He continued to hold it open as Mrs. Comstock approached on her way out, decked in her raincoat, her black, boxy purse dangling from her left arm. "There's a special lunch meeting scheduled at the Main Street Grill for the department heads which I must attend. Professor Meinz said he'd fill in for me until my return. He's running late and will be here any moment. Keep a watchful eye out for that rude Rob person."

As she clomped down the outside steps, Professor Meinz came jogging up. He nodded to her as he dashed past, waving to us. "Hi, Lorie, Ben. See you at the front desk in just a moment." He veered off, making his way towards the Men's room.

"At least it looks like we'll be covered for the afternoon," I said with a sigh.

Ben grinned and plopped on the bench beside the magazine rack, waiting for the Professor's return. I tidied the pencils, and notepads, on the front desk and accidentally knocked over the container of paper clips, scattering them on the floor by my feet. With an under-my-breath curse, I knelt to pick them up, listening to Ben explain to a student about researching some kind of water craft. *Why hasn't the Professor returned? It's been nearly 15 minutes since he rushed off to the restroom.*

207

When the student wandered off, I motioned to Ben. "Hey, why don't you check out the bathroom to make sure he's okay. He's been in there a long time. Something feels wrong."

He shrugged and sauntered towards the restrooms. I sat down at my desk, turned on the typewriter, and was reading the jacket on a new book when Ben breathlessly leaned over the front desk. "He's gone! He's not in there. You didn't see him leave, did you? I saw him go in there. I know I did."

I shook my head. "What could have happened to him?"

The door to Mrs. Comstock's office opened behind me. The stunned look on Ben's face almost made my heart stop. I turned and there stood Rob, his arms folded across his chest. I jumped up from my desk and slipped around the corner beside Ben.

Rob stared directly at me with a crooked smile and eyes gleaming. "Now, let's get down to business. I know you must have the negatives with you. They're not in your house or car and they're not in Ben's either. So, let's save a lot of time and trouble. Just give them to me now and I'll leave. Nobody will get hurt."

I looked at Ben, then back at Rob. "You have the original prints. What more do you want? Besides, those negatives are going back to Uncle Henry."

"You're going to be difficult about this, aren't you?" Rob moved over to my desk and, sitting in my chair, started opening drawers and moving books. He looked up when Ben started backing away. "Ben. You stay right there. If you try to warn anyone, something unpleasant could happen to Lorie. There's nobody to help you this time. The Professor won't wake up for about half an hour. And it will take Mrs. Comstock a while to realize there was no meeting."

208

Rob flipped through files and looked behind drawers, then glanced down and saw the corner of a manila envelope taped to the bottom of the chair beside my desk. I started to speak, but stopped, quickly looking away. He peeled the envelope off, careful not to rip it, then sliced open the top with my ivory letter opener. When he laid the intricately carved opener on the edge of the chair, I inched around the front desk, my gaze locked on the pointed, sharp weapon. As he sat at the desk and held each strip of negatives up to the light, studying them, I crept closer, stopping within arm's length of the chair. He picked up the final strip and smiled as he viewed it. But before he could lay it down with the rest, I lunged for the opener.

I held it above my head as if I were going to stab him. "Put the negatives back in the envelope and step away from the desk."

He laughed out loud. "You really think you can get me with that pig-sticker?"

My face burned with anger. But before I could reply, Rob grabbed my raised arm and forced the opener from my clenched fist. I fell to the floor while Ben dove over the front desk, landing on Rob. My scream pierced the air.

Students in the library swarmed to the front desk, peering over the edge at the cluster of arms and legs struggling behind the desk. A policeman clutching a Billy club in one hand pushed his way through the growing crowd. Three other policemen followed him along with Ben's roommate, Frank, and Mrs. Comstock. The negatives had scattered during the fall and Rob scrambled to collect them as Ben and I struggled to their feet.

"That's the guy!" shouted Frank, pointing to Rob, who was stuffing a handful of the black strips into his jacket pocket. The policemen grabbed him and cuffed his hands behind his back.

"Those negatives are mine," I exclaimed to the policeman who was reading Rob his rights.

The policeman jerked the strips from his pocket and handed them to me. "Thieving wetback," he muttered. "Nothing but dirty animals."

I took the negatives but shook my head. "No. He is not an animal and he is not a wetback. He is a human being. You treat him like a human being or I swear I'll have your badge."

The policeman looked astonished. "Hey, lady, he tried to hurt you. That's assault. And he took your pictures. He's a lying thief like all the rest of them dirty Mexicans. I suppose you want me to let him go too."

"No, you may arrest him, but no more insults. No unfair judgments. He didn't hurt me," I said.

Ben stood up and tucked his shirt back into his pants. Mrs. Comstock elbowed her way to me. "Are you all right, Lorie?"

"I'm fine."

"Well, I want charges pressed against this man for disturbing the peace. Nobody acts like that in my library," she said to the policeman holding Rob.

I turned towards Rob. "Where is Professor Meinz?"

"You'll find him unharmed in the closet off the Men's room. He should be waking up soon," replied Rob. "I'm sorry, Lorie, but I will lose my job if I don't deliver those negatives to my boss. I left your article on the old lady's desk. You know, they'll never let you publish it."

I looked into his eyes, astounded that they showed no anger. "I can't let you have them. I'm sure you won't have any trouble finding another job."

When the police led Rob away, I was certain I would never see him again. I stepped into Mrs. Comstock's office and retrieved my article before replacing the negatives, still clutched in my hand, in their protective envelope.

As the last policeman left the library, followed by Frank, Mr. Meinz walked with Ben slowly from the direction of the restrooms, rubbing his head. "Well, at least they caught him. It's over now, Lorie."

I slowly shook my head. "I wish it was."

Chapter Twenty-Two

Persistence

The next month was depressing. I submitted the article and pictures to several magazines and newspapers but was turned down each time. With all of those rejections, it seemed like I was simply plodding through the days.

One day, Ben asked, "Have you sent it to the N.Y. Times yet?"

"I don't think there's any point."

"Oh, but there is. Maybe you should take Brad's advice and use only your first initial and last name instead of your full first name," he suggested.

I frowned at him. "I already considered that. But I want people to know that I, a woman, researched and wrote it."

He shrugged. "It might just give you the edge you need, though, to get your foot in the door."

****

Less than a week later, when Ben was over at my place helping repair a stubborn window, a phone call came in.

"Hello?" I said. After listening to who it was, I looked over at Ben and motioned him to the phone. "Just a minute," I told the caller. I covered the speaker with my hand and whispered to Ben, "Pretend you're me!" I thrust the phone at him.

He took the receiver and put it up to his ear. "Hello. Who is this?" Then he tipped it slightly so I could listen in.

The male voice on the other end replied, "Joe Schlett from the New York Times. Is this L. Drucker?"

I nodded my head emphatically. Ben paused, a look of puzzlement filling his face. "Uh...yes. This is L. Drucker."

"Mr. Drucker, we received your article on the Whitehead historical flight of 1901 and were interested in it. By the way, what does the 'L' stand for in your name?" asked the voice.

Ben stood straighter and his voice was stronger and deeper than usual. "Well, my first name is actually 'Lawrence' but people call me 'Lawry' for short and so I just use the first initial as an author." He winked at me and grinned.

"A wise idea. Don't want anyone to think you're a woman," chuckled the voice. "Now what kind of flying background do you have?"

"Well, I don't actually fly, but my grandfather was a pilot in the World War I and told me many stories of his experiences. I've always been fascinated with flight and its history," explained Ben, remembering my accounting. "In fact, it was my Great-Grand-father Meyer's journals that brought this whole Whitehead event to light. You see, he actually knew Mr. Whitehead back in the late 1800's."

The voice seemed positive. "I see," he replied. "Can you supply a copy of the journal of which you speak? There have already been representatives from the Smithsonian talking to our editor about your story and we want to have as much information concerning Whitehead as possible."

I whispered in Ben's other ear, "Remind him that the Governor of Connecticut declared August 16th as the official Gustave Whitehead Day, in memory of his inventions."

Ben relayed my message nearly word for word to Joe, who seemed both surprised and delighted.

"We'll draw up a contract for the article, including pictures and have it in the mail tomorrow. Please sign it and send it back so we can get the ball rolling," said Joe.

When Ben hung up, I grabbed him in a big hug, tears running down my face. "We did it! Oh, thank you, thank you," I gushed. Then, impulsively, I kissed him firmly on the mouth. He held me close, and when I looked into his face he seemed unable to quit grinning.

Finally he pushed me away at arm's length. "Remember, it's not over until all the papers are signed."

I brushed my tears away and reached for the tissue box by the phone. "I just hate the fact that they will take the word of a male but if I'd been myself, they wouldn't have listened. That's just not right."

"Well, do you want to get published or not?" asked Ben.

"Of course I do. But think about it. How would you feel if you couldn't do something you'd dreamed about because you were a guy instead of a girl? Why can't my work be accepted because I'm me?"

Ben shook his head. "Oh, some day it will. But it won't be tomorrow or next week."

****

I raced home from work each day, eager to see the mail. The N.Y. Times envelope didn't arrive until almost a week later. I plopped on a chair at the kitchen table and ripped it open, not bothering to unfasten the string at the top, which had been taped shut. The envelope bulged with several pages and a packet containing all the photos I'd sent. I laid them all aside and concentrated on the cover letter:

Dear Lawrence,

Enclosed please find your original article and photos along with a revised copy of the article as we will print it. Our legal department has insisted that we refrain from mentioning the 'Wright Brothers' in connection with it and that it not be placed in the first section of the paper. They also stipulate that it not be printed in any weekend editions. If you agree to these terms, please read and sign the enclosed contract. A check will be sent upon receipt of the signature.

Sincerely,

Joe Schlett,

Associate Editor

My hand shook as I re-read the letter then scanned the edited version of the article. *I can't believe it. All the work and research I did for only three paragraphs on some unknown page buried with the obituaries and want-ads.* The pages drifted from my hands, falling onto the table and floor and I buried my head in my arms and wept.

The knock on the door seemed like someone pounding on a barrel---hollow and far away. However, Ben's voice exploding on the other side of the door brought me out of my stupor. "Lorie, let me in. I've got great news!"

215

When I clicked the bolt, Ben burst through the door into the kitchen. "Lorie, you won't believe it, but..." He stopped in mid-sentence when he saw my red eyes and papers strewn around the room. "What's wrong? Are you OK?"

It was as if I had lost the ability to speak as I thrust the cover letter at him. He lowered himself onto the chair by the table as he scanned the letter. "Those dirty, rotten..."

"It's no use, Ben. It's over. I can't take any more of this. I'm through. Finished." I fell into the nearby chair and stared at the floor.

"No, wait," Ben said as he laid the sheet on the table. "It's not over. I got to thinking about what you said about the Governor of Connecticut naming Whitehead the Father of Aviation. So I called his office."

I rubbed my swollen eyes and looked up at him. "But why would you do that?"

"He was just on his way out to play golf or something and actually took time to talk to me!" Ben's eyes glistened with excitement. "When I told him about your stay in Bridgeport and the research with Uncle Henry, he said he remembered hearing that you had helped resolve that murder in 1912 and found the Whitehead plane in the barn. Anyway, he said he'd make a call to the Editor at the Bridgeport Herald and see that they ran a cover story about your part in solving that crime and about the plane and all. It's your chance to be heard." With deliberation, I gathered the papers from the floor and counters as he continued. "I know it's not the article you wrote, but this story would certainly tell the world what we know about Whitehead, and keep the Smithsonian out of the picture."

I shook my head. "But that Contract was an important part of aviation history and how it all played out."

"I know. And once you are recognized, you can develop that. But for now, you have a chance to get your name out there."

"I can't believe you actually talked to the Governor himself. Do you think he really will talk to the paper about running that story?"

"Sure, why not?"

"Well, at this point, I'm surprised anybody wants to give me a break. I thought Rob would have poisoned everyone against me by now." I stood up and put the loose pages back into the envelope. "When do you think the paper will contact me?"

As if on cue, the phone rang. Ben grinned. "That's probably them now."

"Oh come on, Ben," I said grabbing the phone off the hook. "Hello? Yes, this is Lorie Drucker."

I sat down hard on the kitchen chair, the receiver pressed to my ear, opening my mouth to speak several times, but only answered, "yes, sir" and "no, sir." Ben leaned towards me, hoping to hear some of what was being said. Finally I hung up.

"Well?" Ben enquired, perched on the edge of his chair.

"That was the editor of the Bridgeport Herald. He wants me to send him the article I wrote along with the pictures and then do a telephone interview after he's had a chance to review my story. I can't believe it, Ben. I just can't believe it!"

"I'm so happy for you," he said, standing up and pushing the chair in.

217

"I don't know how to thank you for all you did to make it happen." I stood, walked over and threw my arms around him.

He waited as I leaned back and looked at him. "How about going out for a cup of coffee with me?"

I paused and looked seriously at him. "Well..." Then I grinned. "I can't think of anything I'd rather do."

---The End---

Author's Notes

About twelve years ago, I came across an article claiming that the Wright Brothers were not the first to successfully fly and land an engine-powered airplane, as history tells us happened in 1903 in North Carolina. When the name "Gustave Whitehead (originally 'Weisskopf')"came up as the first to fly in 1901, I discovered an article titled, "The 'Who Flew First' Debate" written by Major William J. O'Dwyer, USAF Reserve (Ret.). Fascinated by his well-written piece about the controversy surrounding who was really the first to fly, I obtained a copy of "Before the Wrights Flew–The Story of Gustave Whitehead" (Putnam's Sons, NY, 1966) by Stella Randolph along with O'Dwyer and Randolph's book, "History by Contract" (Fritz Majer & Sohn, West Germany, 1978). I also borrowed a library copy of Stella Randolph's first book, "The Lost Flights of Gustave Whitehead" which was published prior to the other one.

"History by Contract" delineates the correspondence Major O'Dwyer received regarding his research into the Wright Brothers-Whitehead controversy, along with the famous Smithsonian Contract mentioned in my book. His non-fiction account provides letters, articles and interviews with many witnesses concerning Whitehead's accomplishments in Tasting the Wind. Due to the power the Wright Brothers' faction wields, information concerning Gustave

219

Whitehead has been discounted for years, in spite of Maj. O'Dwyer's and Ms. Randolph's research.

Any information concerning Gustave Whitehead mentioned in my book is as close to fact as I can find. All references to Ms. Randolph's book are accurate and locations in the Bridgeport and Fairfield area are according to maps of the time. The characters of Uncle Henry and his family, the story and people surrounding the murders, and the Stromberg farm are all fictional. It is known that Gustave Whitehead was aided by many children during the trials of his flights and development of aircraft engines. In a letter to Air Sports International, Major O'Dwyer stated that Whitehead's planes were stored in Knapp's barn on Knapp's highway during the 1930's.

There is also controversy regarding the existence of a photo of Whitehead flying one of his planes. It is possible that one still remains, perhaps in someone's attic, or in negative form. It is my hope that this novel will garner at least some recognition and respect for Gustave Whitehead's accomplishments in aviation.

(Wikipedia.com has a fairly complete accounting of Gustave Whitehead and the controversy surrounding him.)

Also a book, "Gustave Whitehead: First in Flight" by Susan Brinchman (Maj. O'Dwyer's daughter) was published in 2015 providing more intriguing evidence of those early flights. (see ISBN-10:069243907)

About the Author

Sue A. Lehman writes from Lower Lake, CA when she's not out tuning and repairing pianos (Allegro Piano Service) or playing tennis. Sue is also the author of *Blindsided* (*Everything's Relative* in e-book form) and *The Rat* (*A Rat Among Us* in e-book form). Both books were published by Sterling House Publisher and are available through her website listed below. E-book versions are available through Kindle and www.smashwords.com.

Connect with Sue:

suealehman@hotmail.com

www.suealehman.com

www.allegropianoservice.org

www.facebook.com/sue.a.lehman

www.twitter.com/suealehman